Snake oil salesman

A neurologist navigates the treacherous
waters of clinical practice

December 30th 2016

Jeremy R Worthington M.D.

Contents

Snake oil.

Snake oil, originally a fraudulent liniment without snake extract, has come to refer to any product with questionable or unverifiable quality or benefit. By extension, a **snake oil salesman** is someone who knowingly sells fraudulent goods or who is themselves a fraud, quack, or charlatan. Wikipedia.

This book is not a memoire nor a compendium of medical conditions, but a recollection of patients and perceptions. A scattershot of brief encounters, which mirrors in a way, the reality of the clinical neurologist.

The times, they are a'changin

I am a neurologist and over the span a 38 year practice, I have seen many neurological illnesses and diagnostic problems. While I hope I have helped some of my patients, the reality is that most people have had to manage their illnesses to a significant degree by mustering their inner strength and stoicism.. Today the specialty is under threat, from runaway overhead costs and declining payments by the oxymoronically named "healthcare" insurance industry. The entire blossoming of this insurance industrial pox is an historic error that has allowed it to interpose itself between the providers and the recipients of medical care.

When I opened my office in an East coast, overpriced professional building, the opening salvo from the insurance industry was fired within a couple of weeks. A representative from Blue Cross and Blue Shield of Massachusetts had an appointment to see me and her message was unequivocal " We are not here to help you as a provider to our patients," she told me, "These are the things you cannot do, when billing as a provider." Then she went on to unveil our 'relationship". When she had delivered her message, I asked " Thank you, but now, please would you tell me what I can do to make sure I get adequate reimbursement for my services ?" Her reply " No that is against our policies." The very nature of insurance companies is to explore the limits of denial of service, slowed payments, minimizing or clawing back reimbursements. It is the perfect capitalist model bringing riches beyond measure to the CEOs but a lot of heartbreak to families, and stress to both the providers and middle class Americans. Good capitalist business model, bad healthcare model. It was standard procedure in those days for the insurance companies to keep changing the requirement for submitting insurance forms. Periodically the rules would be covertly changed then a couple of months would pass and the reimbursements would dry up. The bills were tossed out and there would ensue a panic in the office and a rush to re-submit the charges with the requisite changes, because there were also looming deadlines included in this little trap. These delay tactics garnered savings for the corporations while at the same time, placing increased burdens on the practitioners' staff, and where possible reducing the physicians' reimbursements. Good idea for profit, bad for integrity. Physicians do a lot of unpaid work and there is an expectation of lost personal time. I certainly see now, looking back, after 38 years, the scope of just how much the insurance companies and hospitals got from doctors for free. Most people would agree that the reimbursement took our sacrifices into account and in many quarters it is still a belief expressed in the media and the public that physicians are overpaid. I think today, the insurance people would sum up my opinion, in one word:- "Sucker". That uneasy relationship has now been superseded by Government agencies and the Insurance industry which have simply torn up any notion of "social contract". Now they have developed some ingenious ways of increasing profits and decreasing reimbursements. There are "products" in the health "Market", which all have different terms and requirements. It is very difficult for consumers to figure out the differences in the numerous insurance products. Often this involves prognostication as to their needs or those of their elderly parents, something that would actually require magic. The office staff have to attend meetings twice a month to understand and comply with the Byzantine and shape-shifting regulations . If you want to find out how reasonable health insurance companies are, try forming a Physician's union, you will waken a ruthless, snarling beast with a large bag of dirty tricks . I heard this from a doctor who tried.

Most physicians are hard-working and successful, paying little attention when a colleague vanishes from their ranks, forced out of their profession, when malpractice premiums reach parity with their gross receipts. A vascular surgeon here, an obstetrician there. Doctors believe that being good at their profession, extends to being good at business and politics but most delude themselves . The AMA, medical societies, and the specialty academies have failed dismally to keep their eyes on the professional prize, and have turned into the temple money changers .

I never joined the State medical society. Apart from its high-priced dues, its mission statement emphasized education. There was no reference to the one thing, we absolutely need, in this slow unraveling of our profession, effective political representation. My first visit to the temple of the Medical society was truly a shock. It stands in a Corporate park on a hill in the suburbs of Boston, nestled among well-known leaders of the Pharmaceutical industry. A shiny imposing stainless steel and glass monument set among equals.

In 38 years, I have yet to hear anything resembling effective representation or leadership coming out of this mausoleum.

I heard a revealing story about a little delegation of neurologists travelled to Washington, to lobby a senate leader. His first question, somewhat to their chagrin was " What do neurologists do?"

Hospital administrators seem to view specialists in terms of revenue stream, not as providers of care. Recently as they lost two neurohospitalists, and the consult service collapsed, the reaction was a shrug of the shoulders.

It was hearing a National Public Radio Questionnaire, that set me to thinking I should put pen to paper about neurology and some of my practice experiences.

"What do you enjoy about your work?" Neurologists diagnose diseases of the nervous system and muscles. In a way I see myself as the organ grinder's monkey, sitting on the shoulders of the many great, astute men and women, who, down the centuries , through careful observation, experience and experimentation , have made it possible for someone like me to make an approximate diagnosis, without much more than a history and examination, and a few odd tools of the trade, a hammer for reflexes, a flashlight, tuning forks and pins which can all be found rattling about in bottom of my black doctor's bag. Charcot, Babinski, Varolius, Monro, Magendie, Willis and a host of great anatomists, clinicians, pathologists and neurophysiologists have passed their knowledge down to us leaving their generous gift to future generations.

Granted, over 38 years, clinical neurology is almost unrecognizable with the technological advances in neuro-imaging and treatment, but more than most specialties in Medicine, the history and Physical, "H&P " remains the mainstay of the clinical neurologist. This is what I enjoy, the traditions handed down to my generation.

In training to become a specialist in this field, we learnt to follow an examination ritual.

While it has been observed that residents (registrars in Britain) proceed in an orderly fashion, older, more experienced neurologists approach the exam, selecting and revisiting the relevant parts of the exam, and using the findings to consolidate a theory. No longer! The doctors, across the board are required to cover all the bullet points and mouse clicks imposed by government regulations, so that they can be scored by insurance elves. The more the providers have to fulfill these bullet points and mouse clicks, the more they will provide and less observation, deliberation and treatment planning will follow

The old, tried and true ways are fading to the brave new world of " Patient satisfaction''. The gnomes have finally, after years of talk, realized how difficult it is to actually analyze "quality of care" but "Patient satisfaction" is the low hanging fruit. "Was the staff courteous? What was the average wait time to see the doctor? How easy was it to get an appointment? . Was the office clean ? I found a negative comment at one of those Find-a-doc-websites An unhappy patient commented that my office was dirty, but the same office, cleaned professionally, was given a 5 star rating for a colleague , with whom I share the space. How can one realistically evaluate a physician? Do you want the schmoozing incompetent? Are you dissatisfied with the thorough doctor who presents the facts to the best of his or her ability? Affable incompetents used to do a brisk business.

My key ring sports a brass plate with the inscription " World's greatest doctor" One time a nice elderly lady was channelling the inscription, when she said that I was the best doctor she had ever met. Somewhat tarnishing, this ego-boosting compliment was her diagnosis of Alzheimer's disease. That key ring is more befitting a surgeon's ego than a neurologist's anyway. One time in the office I made a flippant remark to the effect that 'Its all about me!' I meant the opposite but, misreading my quirky sense of humor, the comment was taken at face value, and shortly, I received a book in the mail with a dedication, "Every patient's story is worthy. Perhaps this book will inspire you to look past your ego." I have a few stories to tell that look past my ego. People who have worked with me have asked "What ego? " There is a certain blasphemy in a society where individuality is exalted, but I believe that the great philosopher, Gautama Sidartha the Buddha identified the toxic potential of the Ego. It must be held in check, if you are to provide the necessary care for your patients, but you need to be vigilant, and the exercise can be a Whack-a-mole game. People with large egos are not easy to be around for long and if you are to help patients your ego cannot come into the equation. I know I was not given to academics in my teens.

A late developer, unmotivated? The education I had in private boarding schools in England divided quite early into an emphasis towards the humanities or the sciences. I was drawn to biology. I remember quite clearly learning about the lowly field Buttercup in Botany and was amazed to learn the complexity of the simplest of flowers. When I left school at 18, the best strategy might have been to go to a crammer, because I did not have good enough exam results to get into medical school, and I was told later that no amount of successfully retaking exams would have helped. Crammers are private institutes where they concentrated on getting you through standard O and A level exams . I have no regrets however, about the different road I took. Instead I was tutored by Andrew Packard who was director of the Zoological department at the Zoological station in Naples Italy. He takes no credit for his contribution but he gave me the inspiration that lead me to the road I travelled in life. Scientists from many nations did studies and experiments at the zoological station and there was a particular interest in the physiology of the octopus nervous system. The exposure to that world, the people, the faint odor of reagents, the methodology, the animals, the library full of journals including long forgotten marine expeditions from the past, was wonderful and exciting . There were microscopes and other equipment donated under the Marshall plan. It was leap into a world I wanted to immerse myself in. At that stage of my life, I started to think about the future and decided that Medicine would be a worth-while and challenging profession. Andrew reassured me that you don't have to be particularly smart to be a doctor. I, next, had to plan where to study. Andrew was able to finagle an interview at University College, London. Clearly I was not qualified to enter a London Medical school where competition among first class students from high powered schools, was intense. The interviewers laughed when I left the room. They certainly had not seen such a quixotic candidate before and they would have been remiss to pass over much better students than me, a sybarite from Naples Italy. Afterwards a kind interviewer came out to talk to me and encouraged me, " Look, if you really want to study Medicine, study it wherever you can." and so I did. You cannot predict how a student will ultimately perform. Success certainly goes beyond their academic credentials and I know doctors who went through the best hospital training, who are barely functioning individuals.

'What do you like least about medicine? " Today there is a lot not to like, malpractice lawyers, paper work, stressful working conditions, expenses outstripping income. I find that administrators and insurance companies controlling the authorization or denial of medications and services, comes close, but oddly enough the worst moments that stand out, have been working with bad colds or flu.

There were times when there was just no alternative coverage. You have to be on your game but instead you feel lousy and you are not able to provide adequately for your patient. One time I had swimmers ear, blame it on my affinity for water, on, in, or under. For a while I lost my hearing and had to shout at my patients and have them shout back at me.

I am lost without my glasses. One time I mislaid them and the patient had and to lend me hers and we swapped them back and forth during the visit. A friend called me one morning complaining that she awoke, spinning. It wasn't long before I was seeing a number of patients with vertigo and finally I came down with it myself and was staggering about like a drunk as well as having paroxysms of vomiting. You know they say that someone who treats himself, has a fool for a doctor. We can be in denial as much as anyone. There is head positioning technique, for a different condition called benign positional vertigo, called Epley maneuver. I thought: well what could possibly go wrong, I will try it. I approximated what I thought I remembered the maneuver consisted of, incorrectly, it turns out, and the result was immediate and dramatic: violent vomiting, and abrupt worsening of the vertigo. I could not stand. I can vouch for the fact that it is a really distressing feeling and whenever I get it, the thought flashes through my mind, that if this persists, my career and life is basically over. In reality, vertigo will almost invariably improve after a few days.

A close second dislike is unwarranted interference by "authorities", Hospital policies and insurance denials, that if obeyed are annoying and inappropriate and could, on occasion, amount to malpractice. A nasty trick the insurance companies play, is to fill the prescription ordered then after a couple of months, inform the patient that they are no longer approving the medication. On more than one occasion I have been told that my prescription was "experimental" and they were referring to medications developed in the 50's. I have, occasionally won a skirmish against an insurance company here, a lawyer there. When a lady with a painful foot condition had tried different treatments she came to me and responded to a local anesthetic applied as a patch. Needless to say the insurance denied the prescription, after all, if they don't deny, they have to pay. I had to write an appeal letter to the company and asked them since they were denying a treatment that was working, would they kindly recommend a new treatment plan, knowing full well that they did not have one. They just went ahead and authorized the prescription without responding to my letter. Poison pills buried in my reports occasionally catch the unwary lawyer. One time, I did an independent medical exam on patient with a number of physical complaints and vague, nonspecific findings which were difficult to put together. As the patient had already seen a number of doctors, I decided to go back and review the details of each doctor's physical exams. What became obvious, was that no two examinations were the same, so in my report, I documented all the exams, and commented on this in the conclusion. His lawyer telephoned me to say that he did not agree with my findings! I pointed out that he obviously agreed, then, with my conclusion. I did not challenge him as to what his "exam "consisted of. He was not heard from again.

There is a very lucrative, unscrupulous arrangement that I am sure is identifiable in most large cities and this is the auto accident scam. A lawyer, a doctor and a chiropractor, work together to exhaust the accident coverage to its fullest. This involved numerous chiropractic visits and extensive neurological tests, EMGs MRIs. Some accident patients have even been referred directly to me from a lawyer's office. Now if you were involved in an accident and required medical treatment, I would have thought the first stop would be the emergency room not the lawyers office, but apparently I am wrong about this .

Trip-wires

The city where I practice has a large Portuguese population, mostly, people who have migrated from the Azores, for work, or family. Many like to return to the islands later in life. These are mostly straightforward, working-class people who appreciate their care. Many have a good family support system. The family is often there in the hospital room, bringing   prepared food from home for their loved ones. They used to help me with translation, or a Portuguese-speaking nurse would   help out. After years of this, it was decided   that   professional   interpreters   were necessary and if they were unavailable, there was a back-up telephonic service. This was been ineffective in my opinion, because of the complexities of human interactions and the unnatural matter that this form of communication takes. I read only recently about warnings to doctors that on-line translation may actually cause more errors. On one occasion, I was forced to use a three-way telephonic interpreter. A lady with advanced senile dementia, had trouble holding the phone the right way up to start with, but she eventually mastered it. As soon as she recognized a Portuguese voice on the other end of the phone, she engaged in a lively conversation with someone she presumed was a relative. I did not get far with that interview. If a translator is required, doctors are expected to provide them in the office, at no cost. In theory, every doctor in this area would need to have readily available translators, fluent in Portuguese, Spanish, Korean, Japanese, Cambodian, French, German, Italian. You see, there is no need to know how something works, in order to make laws regulating it.

It seems that today, it is no longer necessary to do the right thing so much as to be seen to have done something….anything! The Department of public Health probably promulgated this and all the systems are now operating fully compliant and fully useless. Just one of the many trip-wires in the day's hospital rounds .

As a young doctor, I had no idea of the shear number of trip-wires that would impinge on my career. Of course, the celebs and professional sports men and women are always being tripped up with much publicity and derision. As a professional, you might imagine that doors would open, rugs smoothed, so that the professional could be used to maximum efficiency for the community's benefit. Not true, of course. There are just countless ways, things do not work . As a resident neurologist in a teaching hospital, one time I ordered an X ray and though this was exceptional, they managed to lose 6 out of 7 requisitions in a matter of an hour or so. Today, now that doctors have signed up as hospitalist, (i.e. employees) there are hospital administrators that tell them what to do and when to do it . A 28 year old administrator told a hospitalist which floor he should start rounding on first! When computers arrived, we were required to use them to view the neuro-imaging. It took up to 20 minutes to access them, Sometimes 20 minutes was not enough and in exasperation I would go to the department, only to be informed that there was a "problem" or an update. No one thinks to communicate with the doctors when these internal changes occur.

In the old days, spinal tap trays were readily accessible in the ward supply rooms. Then the hospitals moved them to central supply. One time I got a consult that I felt would require a spinal tap, so I said " Go ahead and get an LP tray from central supply. Tightening up procedures, the Administration decided a Nurse supervisor was required to get the LP tray. Nurses were not allowed to take the initiative. I arrived 20 minutes later from another hospital and the tray had not arrived. I waited and then went down to the ER myself and picked up a tray, and did the procedure. Eventually the Supervisor arrived with the tray in hand, 45 minutes after the request. It can take 30 minutes to have a hospital interpreter to arrive on the floor. Then to add insult you get questioned as to why a consultation was not seen earlier. I have challenged hospital administrators about their rules at both hospitals I have worked at. If you are going to say a patient must be seen within a certain time frame, then it is obvious you must set limits on how many hours a doctor should work. Having no answer they simply ignore you.

I am wont to say that I spent the first half on my career getting into bad relationships that I spent the second half getting out of. There was a difficult marriage with huge financial consequences. She neither knew nor cared about the vicissitudes of practice and the hard work it took to earn enough to support a family. One thing she was very clear about, she was a doctor's wife and she was never going to work. People assume that doctors emerge from their training pupa stage, fully informed about relationships, finance, investing as well as a broad knowledge of medicine.

We built a New England Salt Box house contracting with an inexperienced builder. It was never completed in 18 years and when I sought legal advice, about how I found myself in this situation, I was told that contracts are only as good as the people who sign them. The builder's opinion was that I could not possibly have been that naive because I was an M.D. Yes as far as I can tell, M.D, comes with a large target sign painted on your back.

I rented office space in a professional building. Again, I was told, before I left training, that this "clinic" was underfunded. I had no idea what the implications of "underfunded " were, and I had to learn the hard way. The physicians in the building supposedly were the owners and the business plan was that, after an initial monetary support, one had to purchase so many shares. These shares did not correspond to the value of the property, Unknown to me, there were many non-physician shareholders in the city, doing nicely from their investment. One was left to one's own devices when it came to practice management. I knew neither about business, nor how to run a practice. Medical students and residents were not trained at all in practice management though I believe that problem is addressed in today's medical schools.

Some of the members of this office building, had originally started small and developed a good reputation in the city, but over time with success and expansion came a dilution of the membership's chemistry. I admit I was part of that dilution process. I did not carry the institutional genome. The structure was not designed as a group or a clinic, but the older doctors on the board, persuaded the shareholders that they were members of an august institute and that they, their leaders, had the ability to tap into the renters for their projects.

When I finally sought legal interpretation of the lease agreement, it was clear there was no such arrangement it was all smoke and mirrors . There was also discovered, about this time, brazen corruption, stirring in the depths, beneath the smooth surface, where the renters bobbed about innocently, like rubber duckies in the bathtub.

I was a member-in-good standing, until the matrix was revealed, then when I stopped paying the surcharges, I became a member in not-so-good- standing.   I tend to bristle now at the concept of good -standing. Who is making that determination?   You see, I think the people who are responsible for the corruption are the ones who are not in good standing. As the debacle of Iraq was unfolding. I could give you a long list of Washington operatives who I considered treasonous to our country. They were responsible for untold harm to humanity and to US treasure and our international reputation. It is not treason if you hold the power though. As Richard Nixon famously said, "If the President does it, that means it is not illegal" So it was no great loss to me to lose the title of Member-in-good-standing.

Two examples of the management thinking from that time, illustrates the process. A project to build a new surgicenter was floated, but, this time there was a split in the membership. Obviously the high rolling surgeons would benefit the most. Some renters did buy in the new building, but others did not. At a board meeting, I attended, one director opined that everyone in the building, whether they were shareholders or not should be responsible for the payment of the project's legal fees. The non-participating shareholders should pay, because 'they deserved it" It was rumored that the proponent of this kept a copy of "The Prince" by Nicolo Machiavelli, under his pillow. He certainly quoted Nicolo, verbatim, rather frequently " They will believe, and when they stop, we will make them believe" The finances seemed to be opaque, so trying to understand what was happening, I asked at a shareholder meeting for the financial statements of the building and the manager asked in open meeting, "Do we have to give him this information?" . That, for me, was the answer; I no longer needed to look at the finances, they were clearly hiding something, and I knew it was time to look elsewhere for a space to rent. When it comes down to it, when people are about enriching themselves, like corporations, ethics, fairness, honesty are tossed. The mantra, you hear all the time, is that their unethical conduct is driven by "the shareholders" but everything I see points to "the CEOs."

Those board meetings themselves gave me a strong sense that a small cadre of insiders engaged in board discussions, before the actual meetings.

Malpractice is a much smaller tripwire than people imagine. Personally, I was named as a defendant in two cases, during my later years in practice and both cases were dropped. Had I gone through a court case or insurance settlement for an actual medical error, judging by the effect that frivolous lawsuits had, I am sure it would have had a much more serious and enduring impact on me. I have to admit that after two cases I was named in, I started to think it was time to retire. These two case came so close together that my administrative assistant came running with the second subpoena in hand, saying "It is time to get out of hospital" . I repeatedly heard that "we" doctors are in charge, we control the patients and where they go et cetera. There is no truth to this. With the emergence of many different types of insurance models, implying exclusivity, and cost cutting measures, the employers jumped off the private practice fee-for-service band wagon, at the first opportunity. I would never have predicted it, after all the struggles that dominated the inner workings of that office building, but it is now essentially run by a hospital administration, with all that that entails.   The administration cares not a jot about conscientiousness and dedication, they care a lot about paying for overtime.

Travels with dementia

Some years ago, I was taking care a Portuguese gentleman who had developed significant memory loss. He had periodic visits to the office with his wife. Then one day she told me, she was going to take him to Lisbon for a visit. Quite often, demented patients are anchored to reality, by their familiar environment, but are out on the high seas in new situations. I cautioned her that he might be difficult for her to handle, once he got there. I don't know how this came about, but a few days later he was back at Boston (Logan airport) alone! . He had somehow navigated his way to boarding a plane back from Lisbon, entirely without help. So much for Alzheimer's patients, they can surprise you! A jet-age homing- pigeon.

When I was in the neurology residency program at New England medical center, Pine street Inn residents were well represented on our floor (ward). Pine Street Inn is a shelter for homeless men. It was remarkable that these gentlemen could not find their own rooms on the neurology/neurosurgery floor, but put them out on the street and they shuffled off south to Pine Street, unerringly.

Recently some Neuroscientists have discovered that we have an internal GPS system. We knew that.

There were empty wine bottles sitting under the street signs outside the hospital. A middle aged gentleman fallen on hard times was in the emergency room, clutching his stomach and told me how ill he felt. He: "I feel terrible, Doc, I just drank two bottles of Champagne," I: "My heart bleeds for you, Sir."

We had a Taiwanese doctor in the residency program. She was very dedicated to her patients and she worked very hard and tirelessly for days, to coax her chronic alcohol patient gradually back to health . The day after he finally got well enough, to be discharged, she was walking up the street in the heart of the "Combat Zone" when she saw the patient, she had lavished so much attention on,   lying in the gutter. "What did you do?" we asked, our eyes widening with anticipation of this good Samaritan's response . "I walk by on the other side of the street." she replied.

Another Portuguese gentleman with Alzheimer's disease was found wandering somewhere north of Boston about 70 miles from home and when the police caught up with him, he explained that he was walking back to Portugal .

A Portuguese lady was admitted to the hospital with a stroke. Later we required a social service consultation, because she had no home to go back to. Her husband had taken the opportunity to vacate their apartment, taking everything with him, while she languished in the hospital .

The other day I was answering an ethical question on line. (more and more on-line courses are mandated by the Board of registration, Hospitals and group authorities) " A woman is in a vegetative state, after a head injury, and her daughter is the only living relative and has durable power of attorney. Do you let the daughter withdraw her care or do you get a court order to continue care?" They are not looking for an answer based on your experience. The correct "answer" is : comply with the daughter's request . My memory however scrolls back to: Head trauma:- notoriously difficult to predict outcomes . While trauma centers are improving their prognostic ability, there are cases, though, that take months to recover even from an apparent vegetative state. The question predicated that the family has the patient's best interest in making a substituted judgment. That is not always the case. I was not satisfied that in this case, that the patient's interests and prognosis had been fully explored.

It reminded me of a time I tried to uphold the patient's interests over the family's. A middle aged lady suffered from a second stroke so that she was afflicted by strokes on both sides of the brain . Naturally this was severely incapacitating. She was able to open her eyes but not move or communicate during the first day in ICU. Very early in the course, her husband and daughter requested that the hospital withdraw her medical support and I arrived to find her being moved out of the intensive care . The nurse in charge was a little affronted by my opposition to the plan. I did not agree with the decision, and I indicated that this would be a suitable case for referral to the ethics committee. A meeting was convened for the next morning around 10 am, which I could not attend because it was in the middle of a long office day and I was given no notice. I suggested we have a meeting at about 6 pm when I was available. No one was willing to come at that time, I think they had a conflict with cocktail hour.

In a confidential chat with the social worker, who was equally perturbed with the developments, I was told that, at the meeting a "religious person" opined that I was merely "grandstanding." Back on the floor, the stroke victim had been moved to a room on her own and was placed on a morphine drip for no more tangible reason as far as I could tell, to hasten the family's wishes. By this time, I could no longer establish any level of communication and in a short time, with a little nudge, nature took its course.

An interesting postscript to this episode, which the ethics committee never heard, was that other family members were on staff at the hospital and were very upset with their decision. They had already contacted a Washington law firm, dedicated to protecting patients' rights. I think that they naturally were hoping to reinstitute supportive care until we had more time to assess the prognosis.

I did witness a euthanasia, when I was an intern. Personally, I felt that a lot more discussion should have taken place. I thought there was rush to judgment, it was a very disturbing experience to witness. That does not, in any way, indicate I am against assisted suicide, I am for it when performed with all the safeguards. People should not have to suffer terrible pain to the last gasp, it is inhumane, but in my limited experience, dying is not usually associated with unbearable pain. The patient with ALS suffers from retaining their full mental faculties while experiencing the progressive loss of muscle strength and ability to breathe. I have watched a documentary about assisted suicide in the Netherlands. While it is disturbing, I still support that individuals right to die.

There was a Portuguese gentleman who was having issues with his memory. He told me that back in Portugal both his sister and mother were institutionalized with Alzheimer's disease. He was scared that he might have the same condition. After examining him, I believed he actually had Huntington's chorea, a much worse diagnosis. The news fell heavily on him naturally and a couple of weeks later I was called to see him in the ICU. He had drunk antifreeze and alcohol. The antifreeze is ethylene glycol, a sweet tasting alcohol results in depressed consciousness and renal failure. Cruelly, it turned out that alcohol (ethanol) is an antidote to antifreeze.

Gods and Docs

Religion is an interesting sideshow in the hospital. After the Portuguese wave of immigration came an influx of sad Cambodians. I don't think I met one family that was not brutalized in one way or another by the dreaded US-backed Pol Pot regime. The Cambodians are mostly Buddhist. I have listened
outside a room for 10 minutes while a group of saffron-robed priests chanted their low monotone prayers to a Cambodian patient . They were very gracious but were not about to surrender the room to a technician like me. There are other Cambodian rituals for the sick, such as coining; heated coins are placed on the chest or used to scarify the skin. That can be a surprising finding, round burns on the chest of a cardiac arrest victim

A young Cambodian lady drowned in a swimming accident. My exam showed that she had no brain reflexes. She was a beautiful young lady in death as in life and it is easy to see how difficult it must be for families and even hospital staff sometimes to let go and acknowledge that brain death is death. In the state of Massachusetts once the determination of brain death is made, the only appropriate action is to withdraw ventilation, IVs et cetera, unless there is a plan for organ harvesting . Imagine my surprise, then, to be on a regular hospital floor, a week later, and find that the patient had been moved there and had been kept on a ventilator, for an entire week after she had been declared dead! It was explained to me that the Buddhist religion would not allow the withdrawal of support. I have some interest in this philosophy and futile gestures are not part of the Buddhist tradition, quite the opposite.

One time I saw two patients on the same medical floor. One was brain dead and the other in a vegetative state. A younger nurse involved with both patients protested my management because I handled the case of a patient in a vegetative state completely differently from the other newly admitted patient with brain death, The difference is not that obvious at first glance and the decisions we make can seem arbitrary which they are, and capricious which they are not. She was on the verge of reporting me to someone in the hospital administration before the difference was explained to her.

The majority of residents in the city are Roman Catholic and the priests visit their parishioners regularly. We each troll the floors doing our work and not treading on one another's toes but when they come trouping, en masse through the intensive care unit, dressed in their head-to -toe black robes, to pay their respects and offer up prayers for a dignitary, that is a different matter. I was consulted as an emergency on such a case. While this panoply paraded by, the head nurse and I made some calls to get the patient transferred to a Boston hospital and were immediately successful.

I was reminded of Fellini's Roma and the clerical fashion show. It turns out that Prayer has been shown not to change hospital outcomes and believe it or not, they have actually done head to head studies where fervent-prayer is compared to prayer-free cohort .Why? You might well ask! During the ICU intercession The Medical director was all of a flutter and quite put out that, without ceremony, we had negotiated a rapid transfer to Boston, where he had failed. I don't think he was impressed overhearing me comment upon their arrival " That is all we need" He did not seem to comprehend that you cannot transfer patients to another hospital, without any information. To him, taking credit is what mattered and he took the credit anyway and that is what V.I.P admissions are mostly about.

I was sitting at a desk at the nurses station, one day when a gentleman arrived on the floor with a large and impressive package decorated with, what I recognized immediately as, the Vatican seal. I lived in Italy for a number of years. Apparently the Vatican sends out such spiritual care packages on request, The emissary had to get a signature for the package but the staff were strangely reticent, and shrank from signing despite the religious affiliation, so I signed it. Ironic that a "non-affiliated" person should sign for the care package, but the Vatican mail must get through.

Uniform semiology

I stopped wearing neckties during my internship and started wearing bowties. It is a habit I keep today and some of my patients are disappointed to find me with a necktie, when they come to their appointments. Recently the British Medical journal has discouraged the use of neckties for the same practical reasons I decided to wear bowties. When I was an extern at St Thomas's across from the Houses of Parliament, I was told off , like a naughty school boy for forgetting to put on my tie, but when I came to the states a student opined it was Un-American to wear ties.

An elderly lady came to my office complaining about a pulsatile sound in her ear and as I was examining her, I realized that she had an uncommon Glomus jugulare tumor which grows into the middle ear and is highly vascular. This is a rare cause of pulsatile tinnitus. Suddenly she collapsed and fell off the exam table and I was just able to break her fall, but as she lay there I could not find a pulse and called a "code" She probably had a temporary slowing of her heart, because she recovered quite quickly and was transferred to the hospital .

By the time I got to see her in the hospital, she was telling anyone who would listen, "I fell for Dr Worthington". I think it may have been the bowtie!

Some Doctors walk the floors with white coats. I do not, but I do understand that stethoscopes, white coats and prescription pads are all part of the Doc props that are important symbols of respect and trust, that is actually part of the treatment. One day I was rounding and had on a dark Navy blue sweater with a round neck which covered my tie. The white collar and high neck gave me the appearance of a priest, at least to the patient, and as I entered the room she addressed me: "Hello Father". It was a time when the sexual abuse scandals in the Catholic Church were coming to the attention of the Attorneys general. When I went back to the Nurses station, I struck up a conversation with a colleague. "I am not sure I want to be mistaken for a priest in this day and age, anyway what is with the priesthood and pedophilia?" He had some interesting insights which were validated by adding that he was both gay and had attended a seminary when he was a young man   Pedophilia is not the same as homosexuality, even if   the Boy Scouts of America conflate the two. He explained that there is a disproportionate percentage of homosexuals in seminaries, because when Catholic families recognize their sons are gay, they   push them towards the priesthood as therapy or atonement ?. The first decision he had to make, on arrival at the seminary was the choice of residence based on sexual proclivity.

Infectious diseases.

My belief in my knowledge, as a new graduate from medical school, was inapt. There are still some things that I occasionally dust off from my memory, but it much more useful to learn to search for information constantly, in medical indexes, medical journals and in recent years, Dr Google. We had no Chikungunya, Zika, HIV, Lyme. I did not realize that I was just on the information On-ramp when I graduated. I think I learnt team-spirit in school but did not learn how to learn until University

In the eighties, a new medical challenge arrived on the scene. Young men were dying of an immune system failure. We were soon to learn that a virus was responsible, the Human Immune Virus . The link between these men was their homosexuality, and it was not long before I started to see some of them. They had moved away for work or life style, returned to the City of their origin to die. There was no treatment, and the complications were florid and overwhelming. They were returning to their families from all over the country. Homosexuality was stigmatized in those days but the Nation has moved a long way since then. There are still horrific atrocities and violence against the LGBT community. The rightwing televangelists went a long way to demonizing them and their vitriol has only toned down after the spread of HIV to heterosexuals. This fact tended to weaken the argument that it was God's punishment for gay men. I have a theory that gays are hated the most by right wing politicians and televangelists because they, themselves, are in a state of panic and denial about their own sexual preferences. How else does one explain the Fire and brimstone evangelists who are eventually outed in gay relationships or trysts.

The first time I saw a patient with AIDS, this was a new disease to me. A colleague told me he had just got his first consultation for a patient with AIDS and later that day, I was at a nurses station, when I perceived , approaching from my right, a young man being wheeled down the corridor, on a gurney. I had never seen AIDS but recognition was immediate, this must be the face of AIDS, thin, and pale, sores on his face, a Hieronymus Bosch portrait of pestilence. The gurney stopped right behind me as they were looking for his room. I felt the presence, then suddenly a hand touched my upper back and stayed there longer than I felt comfortable with, and he said "Hi". Awkward, but also at the first brush with a fatal infections disease, instinctive fear .

I was to see a lot more AIDS and as I became more familiar with its ravages, I was referred more and more difficult cases, with unusual infections and syndromes, I had never seen before. There was a bartender, whose hands were covered in a brown hairy looking eruption. This fell from his palms, when he started treatment for syphilis. All sorts of common organisms are able to access the brain when the immune system fails, viruses and organisms such as toxoplasma, yeasts and fungi. CMV, a common virus can attack the nerves in the back causing weakness and severe pain in the legs. Lymphomas and dementing illnesses are attributable to the Human Immune virus itself. I was fed a steady diet of difficult neurological problems to unravel, by a young infectious disease specialist taking care of these problems. For a while, I felt she and I were comrades-at-arms and just when I thought this was going to be a way of life, managing hugely difficult, time-consuming problems for young men with no insurance, It all came to a halt. New antiviral therapies had come on line.

Eventually, the treatment options became so effective that now, if I see an HIV patient in the office, it will be for an unrelated matter. The AIDS epidemic was very challenging to practicing doctors in the trenches. A new disease, a wide range of devastating complications never seen by the practitioner before, and with an extra twist of little or no reimbursement. When people apply for free care, the hospital is compensated, however, the providers are not. Another example of the social contract gone off the rails

Early in my practice, I did neurological consults every other week, in Newport, Rhode Island. The Psychiatric ward was appropriately on the top floor of Newport Hospital. A lady was admitted in an acute state of agitation and was placed in the padded cell. I examined her there and it transpired that her extreme agitation was triggered when she went to her closet and did not recognize any of the clothes hanging there. Her conclusion was that her husband must have a lover and that the clothes must belong to the interloper. She was quickly remanded to the padded cell to protect her from self-injury. Her examination revealed that she had, an inability to recognize the things she was looking at. She had the deadly Creutzfeld-Jakob disease.   This is a prion disease.

Prions   are   proteins   that   replicate themselves like viruses, but do not have any of the relative sophistication of the viruses, which can insert DNA or RNA code into the cells of our bodies through receptors, then reprogram the cells to start making viruses instead of other normal cell proteins. Prions are proteins that have the effect of a spanner thrown into moving parts of a motor.   These proteins simply fill the neurons with clumps of infectious protein   material, disabling them, slowly and irrevocably taking over the brain. The neurons look as though they are full of cysts, giving rise to the misnomer " spongiform encephalopathy"

When I was in training, a lady presented to the Emergency room with confusion. I found her lying on a gurney leaning on her elbows, with a blank staring expression. She had a peculiar movement disorder, her hands were held in front of her, and her fingers were contracting rhythmically . I could see in my mind's eye, what her brain activity looked like:- high voltage .periodic , sharp wave activity She did not orient towards me as I entered her cubicle, but she was just staring and seemed be blind. She had the same terrifying disease. There is evidence these prion proteins have been transmitted by corneal transplants,   even   inadequately   sterilized neurosurgical instruments.

In Britain a prion disease called mad cow disease became a scare in the mid 80's. It was transmitted to humans in the beef products, It transpires that the cattle feed was contaminated by supplementing it with animal protein from Scrapie diseased sheep. The prion protein transmitted to the cows and then to humans resulting in a Creutzfeldt Jakob-like syndrome. Though the human disease appears to be limited, the prions can still be detected in the tissues of Britons who consumed beef in the 80's. The beef industry has been very resourceful, in Britain by recycling dead sheep and in the US by feeding corn and antibiotics to   cows concentrated in feed lots. What could possibly go wrong, feeding scrapie protein, antibiotics and starch to ruminants? In Italy I recall the beef would shrink visibly in the pan as the steroid-laden meat released its water content. Good profit model, selling water for the price of beef. Bad for people's health .

Welfare & drug abuse

In my experience the middle-class including the medically trained, tend to look down on the welfare class while glorifying the denizens of Wall Street, Corporate Executives and Banksters, who feed off them and undermine the very foundations of a capitalist-based society. I understand the frustration of hard working nurses and other middle class working people but I believe their anger is misdirected against those less fortunate than themselves. It is no "picnic" to live off a welfare check, these "entitled" recipients eat poorly, smoke, and abuse drugs. Over the years I have lost many welfare recipients to drug overdoses. I came to believe through my limited observation   that drug addiction frequently led to death before 40.

One time I mentioned this observation to a patient, shortly after his 40th birthday, and I congratulated him on making it this far. A couple of months later he was gone too.

At area hospitals, incredibly, drug addicts discharge themselves against medical advice with regularity, get a drug hit on the street outside, and promptly request readmission. People will do anything. One entrepreneurial young man, sent his girlfriend out to steal a fire extinguisher from another section of the hospital. She smuggled it into his room where he proceeded to "huff" the contents. I had seen him earlier so I was called back to see him STAT. The nurse first thought he had had an epileptic seizure but by the time I arrived they had deduced that he had been "Huffing " from the fire extinguisher and he was lying curled up on the floor his face and lips, deep blue from lack of oxygen , the extinguisher by his side .. No worry, he actually did fine!

Another observation of mine is that tobacco, alcohol and drug abusers all seem to have iron constitutions. The beating their bodies sustain   before throwing in the towel, is prodigious.

All sorts of debris, ground up Afghan or South American insect parts, talcum powder, bacteria and viruses are injected along with intravenous cocaine and heroin using reused blood contaminated needles. As a result IV Drug users have a range of complications: septicemia, strokes, Hepatitis C, HIV. The toll it takes on the Nation's health and treasure is devastating, not to mention the effect on family and friends. Not all drugs are equal though, Marijuana, the so called "gate-way drug to narcotics" for 30 years has now been downgraded to "gateway drug to alcohol". What next, "gateway drug to pizza? " Most alcoholics would disagree that Marijuana was behind their alcoholism but the guardians of truthiness insist it is a gateway drug to something bad, unless of course there is a sales tax to be had. It seems that the guardians are largely driven by self-interest and include a diverse group from doctors, priests Pharmaceutical companies, politicians and anyone whose business could be affected adversely. There are health hazards from Cannabis sativa but the disorders do not seem to frequent this neurological corner of the woods. After a failed referendum to legalize Marijuana in Massachusetts, I asked "Snow White" a young nurse, how she voted, and she replied that she had voted against the legalization. My follow up question was: "Well tell me, have you ever seen a patient admitted to your floor with a Marijuana overdose?" Her eyes widened, as she could not think of a single case, ever! For the record, I voted for recreational use, however before you photoshop me smoking a giant spliff, for me, it is not about personal use, it is about the targeting and incarceration of African Americans for possession and use . Unfortunately incarceration carries long term consequences that disenfranchise young men, barring them from voter registers and closing doors to jobs, loans, et cetera. Whether this is intentional or not the effect is 21st century Jim Crow.

Over the years, there have been many drug-seeking individuals who show up in the office, most are fairly easy to read. One Monday morning I came into the office to find numerous messages on my Voicemail from Pharmacies all over Fall River .It was as if my doppelganger had stayed up late, feverishly prescribing narcotics willy-nilly all over town. The Pharmacies wanted to know if these were real prescriptions and there was a clue!. The forger had changed my BNDD number (Bureau of narcotics and dangerous drugs) a number specific to each Physician. It was something of a dead give-away. That put a cat among the pigeons in the office that morning.

Almost as bad as when the acting Governor Jane Swift, going over some of her Medicaid bills on Beacon Hill, decided to slash costs by denying payments for Valproic acid. At the time I had numerous epileptics who would have been in real danger if their medication was withheld. N.M.P, (not my problem) apparently, on Beacon Hill. That was another interesting .day in the office

A year or so later the gentleman who had written the opiate prescriptions" called me, actually to apologize but I cut him short, saying I was sorry but I could not prescribe for him any more. His reply, was a little chilling at the time: "Listen, Doc, I can get what I want, anytime I want, have a good rest of your life!" I was not sure how long that was going to be!

Many years ago I inherited a narcoleptic patient getting large doses of Amphetamines, These are tightly regulated drugs but I checked and found the dose he was getting was high but not unheard of. When the DEA caught up with him for selling the drugs, he called and suggested we could have run a thriving business together.

Word is that single-handed Trans-Atlantic sailors needed them and he found a good source of clientele in Newport.

A drug addict in need, is a quick-witted opportunist. One addicted individual walked past my empty exam room where there was an EMG machine. This is a computer sitting on top of a second piece of electronic equipment. The two are held together with Velcro and numerous wire connections joining them. In a fraction of a second he had seen an opportunity and after checking out at the desk, excused himself saying he needed to use the bathroom, turned an abrupt right instead of left , ducked into the exam room and struggled mightily for 15 seconds or less and gave up. We were none the wiser until I went to turn on the machine and found the units all askew and most of the wires pulled out, Incidentally the 40 year rule applied to him too.

The Hospital

When I was in training, we rounded on our patients daily, planning for their management and discharge et cetera. Later in the morning we would round with the Attending physician. One of our patients on a different floor, was ready for discharge. The resident wrote the discharge order. (I think) A week later we were rounding on that floor again and found the patient happily ensconced in her room, getting her 3 meals a day and no visits .

We would troop about following our Attending physician and stopped in the corridors to discuss patient care et cetera. This time our Attending of the month, was holding a pin in his hand as he talked. He liked to gesture with his hands. Next to him, there was a gurney with a water mattress and he, absentmindedly, stuck the pin into it as he chatted. We walked away, as a widening area of damp spread over the cover sheet. He seemed to be unaware of the reason for the ensuing hilarity.

I diagnosed a young lady as having a subarachnoid hemorrhage, when she had presented to the emergency room but the following morning when I rounded she felt well, She was sitting on her bed, cross-legged, smoking a cigarette. I advised her to stop smoke as she needed to be in the best physical condition to undergo anesthesia and surgery. She was referred to a teaching hospital and I heard later that she died on the operating table even before the surgery began. I used to see many more of these capricious, dangerous hemorrhages earlier in my practice, than in later years.

I was called by a young hospitalist to see a patient with Parkinson's disease. He had a very complex drug schedule and had a reasonable quality of life, provided this was rigorously followed. So when he did not wake up from anesthesia, I talked to his wife and ascertained that his medications had been stopped preoperatively, which is standard. Postoperatively he did not resume his medications and because of the complexity, would not be able to take them as previously prescribed, anyway. I came up with a stopgap treatment plan which required low dose dopamine based medication every 30 minutes round the clock. The head nurse agreed that they would do this and within hours he "woke up". I was driving home when I got a call from the hospital pharmacy telling me that I was giving the patient the wrong dose. I suggested that I had spent one and a half hours coming up with this regimen and I would be happy to talk to them again when they had also spent a similar amount of time coming to their conclusion.

3 days later, I was called to come to the floor to see the patient immediately. He had again

lapsed into a coma-like state. On enquiring about the patient's drug schedule, I was informed that they had stopped the medication a day or two before!

A young lady was sitting at a bar and got intoxicated to the point she fell over backwards and had a cardiac arrest. I consulted on her and she has every appearance of brain anoxia. post cardiac arrest with minimal residual reflex activity. I did notice this strange rippling of the muscles, seen only on close inspection. The medical resident asked me what I thought and I told her that, at face value, she was anoxic encephalopathy post cardiac arrest but, because of the fall, anything could be going on intracranially, including a subdural hematoma. Later she went for a CT scan and she had a large subdural hematoma. That was the first time I observed but did not understand the significance of the muscle rippling.

As a neophyte resident, I was consulted on a lady with pain in both elbows. She was being treated for a lymphoma. When someone has pain in both arms symmetrically the cause is likely to be found in the neck and the medical service consulted with neurology with that presumption. In this case I found that she had pain when I pressed on the distal humerus or condyle both sides. The resulting X ray was extraordinary, symmetric tumor deposits in the condyles!

Recently I saw another lady with bilateral

arm pain. She had no pulses. Sometimes you can make a diagnosis of something you have never seen before. No pulses? Must be pulseless disease or Takayasu, an inflammatory disease of the blood vessels.

The hospital had a telephone department when I started practice. I was used to using a beeper from residency, and the doctors used a private answering service. Over time the Hospital department monetized their services and by the time I terminated using their service, I was paying them over $100 a month to answer their calls to me!. Eventually because of the unreliability of a competing answering services I switched to using a cell phone. Occasionally if messages went to the voice mail, they would bubble up out of some phone company server after a few days. Obviously a potential problem but rare, and substantially more
reliable than the answering service. Most of the time, the ward secretaries and nurses were happy to find that when they called, I would pick it up and talk to them. One day on rounds, a registered nurse complained to me "you have a really bad answering service." I told her that there was not usually any problem, but I used a cellphone, not an answering service . Did she dial the number (10 digits) ?. "Oh" she replied, " I could not be bothered to put in all those numbers". Have you ever got dizzy when you encountered this type of response? , In the last 10 years, I noticed I have

been having more and more of these dizzy spells!

I walked in to see a patient who was having trouble swallowing. This nurse was handling him rather roughly as she placed a nasogastric tube and I think she had some doubts about the veracity of his symptoms. She and I, got on well, so she was not offended when I said that she ought to apply to be a nurse at Abu Ghraib. "What is that?" she said "I have heard of Abbey grill, but what is Abu Ghraib?" Abu Ghraib, I will leave you to google, but Abbey Grill was a local restaurant founded by Emeril Lagasse.

Sadly, I was on the cancer ward bringing flowers to a lady I had worked with for many years, She, like many hospital personnel and office staff was a heavy smoker and unfortunately the Piper had come to collect. She was dying of lung cancer. "I know it is my fault, I put myself in this bed".   In a room opposite hers was a gentleman with AIDS. When I arrived at the nurse's station with flowers, the head nurse asked me who they were for, and I told her they were for the gentleman!   It had exactly the effect I was looking for!

Pleased to meet you, won't you guess my name.

I consulted in both City hospitals, one a community, non-profit and the other, a Catholic hospital. Over time, the financial exigencies pushed Caritas Christi to spin off the Catholic hospital to a for-profit company called Steward. Steward is a subsidiary of Cerberus. Cerberus is a private investment company and coincidently the three-headed dog that guards the entrance of Hades. Choices, choices. Eternal hellfire, or being eaten by a three-headed dog. A somewhat sinister name for an investment company but unperturbed, Caritas embraced Cerberus . It has, I am sure only ironic significance, but then Hotel California seemed like a fun place to start with. Anyway, the community hospital across town, though non-profit, seems to be on an identical course with an overpaid CEO and "downsizing" employees. Profit, non-profit?, looks like a race to the bottom .

I digress. The old Catholic Hospital has wards named after saints Joseph and Mary. St Mary's I was quite fond of. In the old days, it was packed with patients, including homeless alcoholics off the street. Sometimes I had to examine these patients in the corridor where they were held in net cages to stop them falling or wandering. It reminded me of the chaos, of the old Pronto soccorso (Emergency room) at St Orsola where I used to hang out after lectures with my Italian buddies. St Mary's eventually was cleaned up and is a very different environment today. What did surprise me was that the three-headed dog from Hades would allow the staff to decide in the designation of the wards and they came up with St Mary, St Joseph, St Domenic, St James, St Jude, St Nicholas, St Antony and Sacred heart. Do I hear the distant rumble of a belly laugh from deep in the halls of Beelzebub? Without realizing it, St Dominic brought me full circle. He was buried at the Basilica named after him in Bologna in 1221, not far from where I lived .

The office

Over the years, I hopped around to different locations to hang my shingle. There was this persistent disconnect, the reimbursements were gradually being eroded and the rents were being gradually raised. Every so often, I would become frustrated by this, to the point that I would look for alternatives. I could see where this trajectory would ultimately go, a tepee or an RV. At the first location, it was suggested that the solution was work harder. Digressing a moment, that solution was also suggested by my Ex wife's lawyer, when he opined in court, that I needed to get a second job to keep his client in the style to which she felt entitled! When the rent went up in the second office, I explained that my income was not going up, but that fell on deaf ears. For a while I moved into an old private building which, at one time, was owned by a Dr Blood. When that became untenable, I moved into a group practice. Unfortunately the costs there continued to increase. There were a thousand little charges (death by a thousand charges) but the rent literally doubling overnight, caught my attention. I was informed that " that is the going rate". For me the writing was on the wall.

I worked with one secretary all my years of practice. Today a neurologist would have a hard time with only one employee. Some need 3, for all today's office and regulatory requirements. Actually most neurologists are moving into academia or research. Some doctors now hire scribes to perform the exacting documentation. The reality is most physicians cannot afford yet another employee on their staff.

There are many components to a doctor office, the staff, the furniture, equipment, answering service, two telephones and in later years computers, flat screens calculators printers, photocopiers, file cabinets. Fortunately I had an accountant to remind me of all the tax payments which had to be rendered on a timely basis and various state requirements. If you do not pay attention to this continuous drain on your business, you will fail. Government loves small businesses, they are the captive cash cow.

I was advised, very sincerely, that the 3 A's were the key to success in private practice. Availability, Ability and Affability. Now I have this little peeve with many of the inhabitants of the home of the brave, there seems to have a problem recognizing irony and hypocrisy. I rest my case with the 3A advocate, who possessed none of these qualities . Someone told me to make sure I signed medical records on a timely basis. Who was consistently at the top of the procrastinator list? You guessed it. A good experienced executive assistant is crucial, more than ever now with the constantly changing but highly complex process of running an office. At the end of an office day, when I finally get home or start preparing some supper, I think that so much happened that I could write a book about just that single day and the cast of characters that pass through or work there.

With the change of seasons, some people dressed for Halloween, We had a lady come dressed very convincingly as the devil, another as a fairy with lacy wings. I usually wear a black and white tie with skeletons dancing on it. I do have some misgivings but fortunately I am not dealing day to day in terminal illnesses, which would have given me pause.

An elderly lady came to the office a little flustered and dying to tell me her story. "Do you know what my tenant upstairs has?" "Sure", I replied "A python." "How did you know?" I had no idea, of course.

Opinions differ about the appropriateness of Doctors and patients discussing religion and politics. I usually steer clear of religion and I accept the blessings bestowed on me as gracefully as I can but I equivocate to direct questions. I found it a little harder to avoid talking about politics. Most of my patients are as I have mentioned elsewhere, blue collar workers. I did have a nice gentleman who was a regular visitor and we always bantered back and forth, amicably about our political differences. One gentleman I do recall never came back after the following episode. I was discussing his condition and he was quite opinionated about what he felt his problem was, which did not make sense to me, At some point he deduced my liberal tendencies and said " You must be a liberal" I replied " Yes, and you must be a republican." " Why." he asked. "Because you hold fact-free opinions." He was not pleased with my retort and suggested in two words that I might have been born out of wedlock. I actually expected him to come back as he definitely had a problem and I do not provide care based on class, wealth or political preference.

You might think that I find insurance companies are a big obstacle in the office practice but despite all the overheads and reimbursement issues, the single greatest problem financially, is the high rate of no-shows. We started our office at 8 am until the last year. Our patients came up with numerous reasons as to why they could not come, illness, flat battery, ride did not arrive, no baby sitter, appointment with another doctor. People would actually say they were in the lobby, downstairs but never arrived. The winner was, " I am still in bed" at midday!

I did a consultation on a gentleman in the hospital and recommended he follow up in the office for testing. My secretary tried for days to get hold of him, and when she finally did reach him, he said" I am not coming " He told her he had been to Boston and I had made the wrong diagnosis. Wait !, What?

This elderly couple shuffled into the

waiting room took one look at my secretary and me, realized we both had colds, turned round and shuffled away, never rescheduled, never came back.

One time, I was driving to work when an overzealous young policeman came roaring up behind me at high speed, lights flashing. I pulled over, assuming he had been called to an emergency, But actually he had divined wrongly that I had been speeding. I denied it and it was true I had driven the speed limit but he had been unable to pass an elderly driver who was driving about 20 mph and had been unable to figure that into his calculation. Anyway, he had nothing to support his contention and had to let me go. Now I had recently been to Costa Rica and while there, ran into a corrupt traffic cop, who stopped us. He, then walked about 50 ft behind the car with my wife, to examine her documents, This charade went on for about 10 minutes, so eventually I unbuckled my seat belt and got out, whereupon he immediately claimed he had stopped us because I was not wearing a seat belt. One of those annoying things, that are usually settled with the green poultice in Central America. He was forced to let us go. I was not pleased to be stopped under false pretenses in either country and I drove straight to the local police station and marched in yelling at them, "What do you think this is? A third world country?" just as Officer Zeal, the police officer returned to the department.

I was recounting this tale to my secretary some weeks later and as I looked into the waiting room, there he was, Officer Zeal himself! When he came into the office, the first thing I said was "you are the officer who stopped me for no reason." An awkward moment for him.

Another police officer was from a nearby town and I told him I had a friend who detours round his town instead of driving through it because of the reputation of the police. He said' Well do you think that is that a good thing or a bad thing?". "I think ...it is a bad...thing!" I replied.

The Pilgrims arrived in the Mayflower on Cape Cod in 1620. It surprises me how often I run into people in Southern New England who are related to some of the original pilgrims. A personal friend, on Martha's vineyard, an ICU nurse.in the hospital . Only the other day, I was checking out at the local supermarket, and the lady at the register told me that she had ancestors who came over on the Mayflower. I said " You, New Englanders don't change zip codes much, do you."

The shopper in line, behind me said, "My relatives came on the Mayflower too!" My Vineyard friend was related to Mr Howland, who fell overboard, while the Mayflower was lying ahull, during an Atlantic storm. In the office, I have seen a relative of the great Navigator Ferdinand Magellan. Another patient was related to Sitka Charley, who was a guide for John Muir in Glacier Bay, Alaska. A patient told me that that when he was a small child, his father pointed out Lizzie Borden as she passed by in a carriage, while they were visiting the cemetery. Lizzie needs no introductions!

I was invited to be on the newly formed Ethics committee at the community hospital. We had a diversity of members. We met periodically but in the end, disbanded when the lawyers decided this was their purview. One day there was a meeting for Hospital social workers in Sturbridge. A speaker was unable to attend so I was asked to fill in. I really had no canned lecture and I am not a good public speaker but, I felt that when people engage in work where serious ethical decisions will develop, they should spend some time determining their own values so when that challenge comes , they are forearmed and ready to employ the values without having to think on the fly.

I have tried to do this myself with medical ethical questions posted on line and they can be very difficult to apply predetermined values to. Still my message was that personal ethical values should trump institutional ethics. This caused some harrumphing among the supervisor class. My reasoning is that history does not look kindly on those who " were just obeying orders" Now, many years later, I feel that institutional ethics have won, the employees are cowed before the All-powerful God Lucre If you fail to bow to the institution today, you will not be seeing your paycheck at the end of the week. So many doctors now understand the contract trap set by hospital administrators.   When I went through medical school and training there were a bewildering number of eponyms to remember. This was a legacy, if your name got attached to a new disease or a physical sign. On two occasions, I have witnessed a sign, that has not been described, and I thought about writing a brief summary. Both patients were comatose and demonstrated, on close examination, some diffuse fine rippling movements in the muscles. I fancied the sound of "Worthington sign".   On both occasions the patients were in the process of brain herniation, the brainstem being crushed from above by pressure inside the cranium. Not a very helpful sign, most of the time, though in these two cases, classic signs were temporarily obscured. The implications were so bad, I could do without Worthington's disconnection sign and I never reported it. No eponym for my CV. If you like though there is also Worthington's law: " He who possesses the power shall abuse, him that doth not" Though generic, it is applicable to today's docs.

There are two kinds of doctors, those that treat their patients and those that treat themselves. Over the years, there have been a number of sudden doctor disappearances, from the roster. Some of the more adventurous, had impregnated young nurses but there were some frauds as well, doing sham procedures or a high number of interventions or just old fashioned insurance fraud.

Non-compliance.

"Keep a watch also on the faults of the patients, which often make them lie about the taking of things prescribed " -Hippocrates , and bear in mind, that he died about 2300 years ago.

I recently heard on the radio that older patients are non-compliant with their prescription medications. Non-compliance is so pervasive that I was ready to do a study on it. I would have to say that hardly a day went by in the office that, there was not a compliance issue. When a patient sat down I would ask if there were any problems with the medications, side effects, et cetera, Then I would ask them to explain what medication they were taking and when. In one case, a patient got so incensed with my asking the same question every visit, that she left and went to another physician. The problem was every time I asked, she did not know. I would give patients a schedule of how to increase their medications. This particularly applied to Parkinson's disease medications. Quite often after a while they reverted to a standard suboptimal schedule. I felt something needed to be done and thought an alarm system combined with a pill minder would be the way to go. Now I have no idea how to begin a project like that and as soon as I conceived the idea, various electronic devices came onto the market. Compliance is much more complicated and now there are telephone-assisted reminders. A pharmacist has suggested microchips in every pill so that compliance can be determined with absolute certainty and I am certain it will identify 100% non-compliance. I have had the personal experience of dose changes and same color pills. The mail order prescription plans may start with one brand, change to a generic of one strength, replace it with 2 pills of half the strength , change to another generic and if you are not compulsive it is easy to jump back to a previous habit . You could be taking 2 pills of a higher dose or one pill of a lower dose. The electronic medical record did do one thing reasonable effectively when used skillfully. It identified non-compliance and doctor shopping and my administrative assistant was a terrific sleuth when it came to patients habits, not refilling their meds for months and using different pharmacies et cetera.

Electronic medical records are really good at required documentation of useless information.

The Tower of Babel principle of EMR building starts with a foundation on sand, then builds to the specs of a software engineer. When this turns out not to work for the doctors, demanding unnecessary work , obstructing the smooth, reliable flow of what does need to be done It gets sent back to administrators for revision and adjustments, They add additional windows for procedures, test results, internal Email, notifications, patient education forms and so on and so forth. As the medical B.S. tower climbs, ever higher, festooned with add-ons, it becomes more cluttered, counterintuitive and unstable. To find a result you may have to click on some random dot and when it opens there is an Aladdin's cave of even more mouse clicks. Watch out though because there is an algorithm, you must do this before that and go back to square one, in the event you forgot a step. If you get it right though, you will need to open some random appendix that confirms that what you ordered was in fact ordered. That of course does not mean it was actually ordered because maybe that will be several more clicks for confirmation. There is a log , if you can find it, that will tell you, if your prescription "went through". My administrative assistant, would check it regularly, under the correct assumption that I had not completed my mouse click drill. Why isn't there a log of the log? The closest I ever got to an answer was eye rolling.

As I was training for EMR's, I used to call it "Death by a thousand clicks" Unfortunately, prescient. So all this creates a rich field of errors for vultures to pick over. The inexperienced assistants just throw up their hands, doctors become frustrated and angry. The wealthy ones hire a scribe.

By now the tower of Babel is looking more like the leaning tower of Pisa, set about with a jungle of vines and strangler figs. Eventually the system is so unwieldy, it can no longer be modified, it is scrapped and the cycle starts all over, with the design engineers and insurance companies and pharmacies administrators IT techs, and when it is ready, they roll it out and the doctors and staff have to spend many hours learning their new creation. It is your worst nightmare. Of course there really is not enough time to teach you everything, so they teach you just enough to get by, until you run into a snag. Then they explain some other byzantine move or they go away and start adding more "stuff". The office staff are often not highly-paid or well-trained medical assistants and mostly they have to learn on the go, so they make mistakes that result in something as simple as a duplicate chart. When that happens you are blind to all the information in the second chart. All this and administrator interference increases risk and better pickings for vultures.

See how easily you got through that without thinking about the impact all this has on patients, doctors, executive assistants and the overhead costs?

Mess with women at your own peril

A gentleman had quite severe Parkinson's disease and was entirely dependent on his wife. He was also prone to be physically abusive to her. We discussed this in the office and she indicated that she had the situation under control," So, how do you manage the situation?" I asked, " If he is threatening, I just withhold his medication!" She used to titrate his medication to keep him from harming her, while at the same time continuing to provide him with the care he needed.

I heard a ward secretary saying untrue things about an Iranian doctor and personal friend. When I asked her why she said these calumnies, she replied " I don't like him,"

A new doctor was throwing his misogynistic weight about with the secretaries, nothing was said but they were not resting, day by day his billing was getting delayed.

One time, I was at the nurses' station, where there was a group of nurses chatting, maybe it was about education. I commented that we were in the age of the ascendancy of woman, whereupon, they, with one accord, attacked me, without, apparently, reflecting on what I had just said.

I hope that I have treated nurses with the respect, they fully deserve and I think I behave appropriately. I do like chatting with young nurses, they have so many issues with relationships and for me that is all ancient history. One time, though, I was performing a spinal tap along with a Portuguese Supervisor, who called herself "Greenhorn nurse" and a new nurse graduate ,who was to assist me. This young lady was impressively beautiful with Rapunzel-like braids, and I found her very distracting. The tap was not easy and after I finished, the supervisor sidled up to me, rolled her eyes and said. "I saw what was going on there".

Bed and bedside manners

As a physician, I have cultivated being indifferent to criticism and praise, as you cannot allow them to influence your judgment. I used to do EMG testing. This can be a somewhat unpleasant test. A needle electrode is inserted into different muscles to determine information about muscle and nerve disorders. The pain can be significantly reduced using small Teflon coated needles . After lying in an exam table for a while, receiving needle jabs, an elderly lady had had enough, and told me in no uncertain terms that I was hurting her, and that I was doing it purposefully and that I was enjoying it. It is not as though I was standing over her with a Cheshire-cat-like smile. I certainly did not like the implication and if there is one thing I do not appreciate, it is having a patient put words in my mouth or tell me what I am thinking. After examining one of my patients, I met the husband in the corridor and he was clearly flustered. "You know doctor, she is all upset because you called her an F... B...! I thought about the accusation, "You know what, I would never say such a thing to a patient, never have and never will. I might think it, but I would never say it." It surprises me how often, I meet former patients who attribute to me, statements which I could not possibly have made because they are completely inconsistent with long held values. Another patient said to me " I know you don't believe me because you think I am fat." She took the liberty of telling me my opinion and I discharged her forthwith suggesting she see another doctor. This is not a trivial matter. She was declaring that I was breaking trust, but it is immaterial, really, where the break came from, you cannot have a Doctor-patient relationship under those circumstances.

One day I cancelled my office due to the flu. A lady called and said she wanted to talk to me and when she heard I was ill, informed the secretary that she was going to sue me because I was perfectly well the day before! A patient was having recurrent dizzy spells which were due to poor circulation in the back of her brain and she was at risk for a stroke. I talked to the patient and expressed my concerns to her and the attending hospitalist, but later after I left , she worsened and the hospitalist called me and we discussed her management over the phone. The following day, fortunately, she was stable but her son following me out to the dictation room, and proceeded to express his disappointment that I has not returned immediately the night before. When I enquired as to what outcome he expected from that, he said "Empathy". "Oh," I replied. "We do not do empathy consults here. "

Empathy is an interesting concept, it is a

constant refrain in theoretic treatment plans, by such luminaries as the Board of Registration who grumble about empathy, or rather, lack thereof, gloriously oblivious of the people-in-glass-houses aphorism.

When a family member came to ask my opinion about her sister's condition, I was still trying to pinpoint the diagnosis but I gave her my honest opinion although I did not tell her I was suspicious that she had a spinal cord tumor. She wanted to know if I thought her sister would ever walk again. I was struggling to put her disorganized test results together. The results were in different hospitals and locations and because of this, I could only access some results on my computer at home, others in the office and still others in the hospital, In order to compare the images , I had to photograph them on my iphone then compare them side by side. My fear was that things were going to get much worst and I told her that I did not feel that her sister was likely to recover. The following day the patient's husband was sitting in the room, all upset that I had not shown enough "empathy" in explaining to his sister-in-law , about her prognosis. If you ask for the truth, don't expect truthiness. Maybe he would have preferred: " Hello I am Dr J, your doctor for today and everything is going to go very well, trust me, OK." She died about 3 months later. Empathy where it is due, like love, do not feign empathy. This episode was upsetting on multiple levels not the least because, I had personally experienced electronic medical records accessibility rise to a zenith and then witnessed its decline to a non-functioning nadir. The problem perversely, appears to be unbridled competition. For a number of reasons, I found that IT personnel either at the hospital or at the office, had little interest in solving these problems. So much for EHRs making communication, information and jobs easier for doctors.

I have become very attached to some of my developmentally disabled patients over the years. Many reside in Group homes. One of these gentlemen had a troubling dyskinesia from prolonged administration of antipsychotic medications, which he had been prescribed for years to control his outbursts. Slowly over several years I was able to significantly improve his involuntary movements, then suddenly he was gone, sent elsewhere. It turned out, as often happens, a new caregiver, a young nurse with little experience but new authority, decided that I was "doing nothing for him."

Most of the time, one is providing maintenance of care to the group home population. Of all those, I have seen and treated over the years, for seizures, only two stand out to me, as successes. Both went from intractable seizures to a level of control where they were able to assume a life with a significant level of autonomy. One lady had been cloistered away from education and opportunity by her family, in all likelihood because of misplaced family shame Over time , little by little, the seizures improved to the point that I pushed her to avail herself of rehabilitation services, and she was eventually able to work , even marry and today has maintained a significant level of independence. The other person remains an enigma, but he also improved to the point that he was asking me if he could get a driver's license. He used to have one minor seizure after another, which could easily be missed by the casual observer. Though not very obvious, these minor seizures disrupted his thought processes and attention continually. He actually carried a piece of paper written by his previous doctor saying " Do not admit this patient. " In today's world, if he shows up he is more likely to be admitted to the ICU, undergo an MRI and several EEGs and blood work, et cetera. Unfortunately, after a period of doing well there would be some new set back like Guillain Barre, and In the end I sent him to a teaching hospital hoping they would uncover some metabolic or genetic cause for his inexplicable reversals. That did not happen but he interpreted it as my abandoning him.

The mentally retarded, developmentally delayed, disabled, mentally challenged, handicapped (or whatever PC label is in vogue) , at first encounter, seem to be a homogeneous group, but as soon as you are exposed to them, you learn how different they all are. Some have very endearing personalities. The young ladies in the office are very happy to see them and fuss over them, even though they may be giving forth volubly, in the waiting room to an audience not used to their antics . I am impressed with the patience and dedication of the staff that bring these clients for their appointments.   I have also learnt how dedicated the parents are, to their well-being and how they fret over them constantly. I have one patient who I have seen since I started practice. She used to come all the time with her mother who never stopped worrying about what would eventually happen to her daughter. To me, she was passive and completely dependent on her mother. The anxiety was a constant in her mother's life "What will happen to her when I am gone?" she used to say. Her mother probably never stopped worrying from her daughter's birth until her own demise, but after she died, the patient moved into housing , met the challenges of every day and now has a significant level of autonomy and comes unaccompanied to her appointments .

I was in the emergency room, one evening, seeing a young lady with developmental delay and seizure disorder. She was in a residence somewhere to the north. Her family noticed that her "seizures" seemed to get worse whenever they brought her home by car for weekends, holidays et cetera. The further she was from the residence, the worse the seizures became. Bringing her home for holidays and weekends seemed to result in repeated medical dramas, that culminated in the ER and that is where I came into the picture. I concluded that she was not having seizure activity, that the only logical explanation I had for her behavior was her fear was of being separated from her perceived life-line, her security at the institution. As the distance increased, the more insecure she became.

I got my neurological training a stone's throw from the Pine Street Inn, a very worthy charitable institution caring for Boston's destitute men. Doctors are not exempt from the lure of the demon in a bottle either but alcohol is never served in hospitals on this side of the Atlantic. The abstemiousness is overplayed. You hear pontifications about the dangers of alcohol in teens putting them at higher risk of alcoholism in later life, and yet, in Italy where little children were well behaved at the table, wine was an integral part of the meal. When I was an extern at St Thomas Hospital, in London, there was a common room where medical students and doctors could buy beer. Quite civilized. I think it is much safer when alcohol is demystified. I cannot imagine that happening here. The Aussies, who will not pass up a cold Forster's, say of the U.S "Thank God they got the Pilgrims and we got the convicts " When I interned in England, the elderly patients were allowed a little tipple at the end of the day upon request . The famous Brompton cocktail was greatly appreciated by those in terminal care. It was a cocktail of Heroin, Brandy and chloroform water with cocaine and Chlorpromazine. I have been told that recipients will not part with even a drop. At Christmas, the wards and Doctors common room were flooded with alcohol. My first Christmas on a surgical unit was more like a bacchanalian feast than a hospital. We used to get a quick pint across the road at the local pub, after working in the operating theater, and before the last call.

Raining People (instead of   cats and dogs.)

It was the middle of the night, the telephone rang, "Your patients has just vomited up some blood." I ran over to the ward, about 100 yards away. There was a rapidly spreading lake of blood under this unfortunate gentleman's bed. We frantically tried to stabilize him but requests for blood were denied because there was also an obstetric   Department   which   required   an emergency reserve at the Blood bank. We ran fresh frozen plasma in as fast as we could. He died just as a nurse came running with a couple of units of packed cells. In those days trauma patients were sometimes admitted to the general ward for observation. There was one unfortunate case, a patient who was transferred to a general ward without stabilizing the neck fracture, not the sort of thing I had training in and not suitable to be handled in a general ward. A physical therapist came running declaring authoritatively that we should all step away from the bed, as she was trained in managing these types of patients. She rotated the patient according to her training and the outcome was immediate, the patient went into respiratory arrest.

A young lady in her late teens was admitted to me with spontaneous bruising spreading all over her body (purpura) .   She rapidly went into shock and died within 6 hours, of the first symptoms. All our efforts were futile Her blood cultures shows she had meningococcal septicemia but clear spinal fluid. A case of Waterhouse–Fridericksen syndrome.

I was in the ER, seeing this lady who came in with " the worst headache "of her life and concluded she had a burst blood vessel (aneurysm) and proceeded to give a report to the chief resident . Being a detail-oriented person, he asked me about the physical findings and specifically asked Did she have a gag reflex? " I said that I did not and would not check, so he grabbed a tongue blade and flash light. It turned out she had a very vigorous gag reflex and promptly died. I guess in today's parlance that would be one click short of a complete exam.

During my internship, which consisted of running from one problem to the next, I had two critically ill patients admitted at the same time. One was in severe respiratory distress, so I instructed the nurse to start oxygen, while across the way, I started to perform a spinal tap. on a trauma patient. As the needle penetrated the meningeal lining, I watched in horror as the spinal fluid went up and up and, then flowed out of the top of the manometer and ran down the outside. I glanced across the ward, just in time to see the other patient slide into unconsciousness. The oxygen had simply suppressed his air hunger and allowed the carbon dioxide to increase in his blood, which at a certain level acts as an anesthetic (CO_2 narcosis). The neurological patient turned out to have bilateral subdural blood collections pressing down on his brain and he was sent to a London Hospital where he was operated immediately. The Registrar called to inform me that all was well but a few days later, the unfortunate patient had a massive blood clot in his lungs and died . When people are hospitalized and are confined in bed for a few days, particularly after surgical procedures, they are at risk for developing clots in the leg veins. These clots are soft and because there is no significant inflammation, they are easily dislodged and break off. A large clot will travel until it arrives at the lungs where it lodges in the pulmonary artery. If it is big enough, it can result in sudden death. There are very active protocols to preempt this terrible complication.

Percival Potts, a surgeon at St Bartholomew's Hospital in London described a series of cases in his " Nature and consequences of those injuries to which the head is liable from external violence' published in 1768 " Case XVI concerned a sailor on board the Southhampton, a British Man-of-war which was in an engagement with
" a fameful fuperiority of French force "A

> failor received a fevere blow on his head by a large fplinter."

He eventually was transferred from Gosport ,on the southcoast, to St Bartholomew"s in central London. Potts consulted on the unfortunate man and operated finding the skull, carious. In the postoperative period, he was stable for several days when

> "of a sudden he was seized with all the fymptoms of peripneumony, and , on the third day from that seizure, died ."

Peripneumony may be an 18th century term for pneumonia but "seized" is not a term I would expect for pneumonia and suspect he had pulmonary embolism. Today we have a number of measures to reduce the risk of pulmonary embolus but in Mr Potts time, blood letting was a standard of care, and one has to wonder on the possible effect of blood letting on pulmonary emboli.

Prolonged air travel puts people at risk, this is why passengers are encouraged to get up and walk about the cabin or do leg exercises in place. Incidentally, St Bartholomew's Hospital is in the "city" of London.

I spent one summer immersed in the hospital life as an extern at St Thomas Hospital, taking the first tentative steps to examine and become comfortable with patients. The first physical contact, is a big transition, crossing a social taboo, if you think about it. This sense of taboo is still with me, when examining middle-eastern women. Patients perceive very well, your lack of experience. I have had smart young medical students sit in, on my examinations and I find them almost as tentative as I was. I make sure to reassure them, that they are doing just fine and I am confident they will become effective in their bedside manner, because they will figure this out for themselves, face to face. It will become second nature and they will get to that point on their own. There is so much to think of just in terms of the details of a physical exam and if you are concentrating on your exam procedurally, it distracts from the signs you need to find and the personal interactions that represent bedside manner .

A fear I used to have was making gaffs. Sometimes one can be so inadvertently hurtful. I felt really bad the first time this happened. There was young mother with breast cancer who was suffering from intractable bone pain. She was being admitted to the neurosurgery team at St Bartholomew's as a candidate for palliative pain management. She was young but looked old and tired and I nervously I referred to her husband as her "son" not once but twice.

There is a genetic disease in the Portuguese population called Joseph's or Machado's disease. My first secretary was admonished ahead of time, by the family of an older woman, to make sure there was absolutely no mention of "Machado's disease" which she was very frightened, she might have. "Do not mention Machado's disease under any circumstances". I was seated behind my desk, when my secretary opened the door and introduced her, " This is Mrs Machado." Her expression mirrored her horror at the words that had just spilled from her lips. I think the poor girl wanted to die in that moment, but the visit actually went fine. Another time, I made a telephone call and enquired if the husband was home. "That is me" he replied in his high pitched voice. Jerry Seinfeld did a spoof about this in one of his shows. As men and women age they seem to converge in outward appearance. When you run into Mr Raposa, it is embarrassing when you address him, as Mrs Raposa. There is just nothing you can say other than "Oh God, why did I do that ! "

Tricky business

Occam's razor, is a philosophical principle
whereby when faced with competing hypotheses
one should choose the hypothesis that employs
the fewest assumptions. I think maybe William
of Ockham never visited my neck of the medical
woods, where Multiple Sclerosis looks like
Machado's disease, or Lyme like Lou Gehrig's.
The young lady with a history of Migraine
headache, who after so many migraine attacks,
presented with a cerebral hemorrhage. The
classic "combined system degeneration (B12
deficiency) that turned out to be spinal cord
compression . The Parkinson's patient, who
developed muscle wasting and actually had
Machado's disease. The patient with Parkinson's
disease, who actually had an epidermoid tumor.
The patient who had Temporal arteritis, scalp
tenderness and all, which turned out to be an
acute subdural hematoma. There are so many
snares and diagnostic booby traps for the
unwary. I am always challenged by patients who
have two or more illnesses confounding the
traditional physical exam.
I identify more with Hickam's dictum , and if
you were to read the medical coding, spewing
forth from doctor's offices today, you would
agree that the medical profession has fully

embraced Dr Hickam and his dictum .

Hickam's dictum "Patients can have as many diseases as they damn well please".

Both Hospitals I work at, have modernized but when I started, one ward had old creaky wooden floors and rattling cast-iron steam radiators, a subdued light filtered down from fixtures in the high ceilings. The other hospital had some old dark wards with bars on the windows, at the far end of the institution. Often the most interesting patients were to be found in these dingy backwaters. There was at some level, a class designation to the ward assignment. I sought out a patient in one of these locations for a second opinion. She was having some difficulty walking and had signs of Parkinson's disease, so I started her on Sinemet which basically delivers the neurotransmitter Dopamine to the brain. She got better. The first consultant's opinion was that, yes, indeed, she did get better but it had nothing to do with the medication she was prescribed! This is called escalation of commitment

The principle that underlies the pharmacology of Sinemet is beyond the scope of this story but is worth exploring. It is really remarkable that one can swallow a pill that delivers a neurotransmitter that acts upon nerve cells and reverses some of the symptoms and signs of

Parkinson's disease.

An aerial acrobatic was flying his plane high over New Bedford when he suddenly developed dizziness and blurry vision. He made it safely down and was admitted to the hospital for tests. He had, by then, developed paralysis down one side which improved and was then followed by paralysis down the other side. At this point he was dismissed by the doctor as an unreliable historian. (Confirmation bias) His symptoms continues and I was called as a second opinion. It turned out he had poor circulation in the Basilar artery supplying the brainstem and that was why he could not "make up his mind "which side was affected, because intermittently, both sides were. That was a close call for him and the city of New Bedford.

A gentleman was having some dental work when he appeared to faint in the dentist's chair but he recovered quickly and was sent to the hospital for a work up. Initially I thought about the usual low blood pressure, slow heart rate et cetera. As I was writing my report, I recalled an experience that happened to me, so I stopped my dictation and reentered his room, asked one more question, and his answer gave me the diagnosis.

Dentists sometimes use a syringe with a long thin somewhat flexible needle to reach the mandibular nerve where it enters the jawbone. The glass vial containing the local anesthetic, has a non-detachable needle. When injecting, we normally pull back a little on the plunger to see if the needle has penetrated a blood vessel, but you cannot do this with this type of syringe. Years before I had been to a Harley Street Dentist's office, (complete with Persian carpets). When he tried to inject the local anesthetic, I had a momentary intense dizzy-faint feeling. When he started working on the cavity, it was clear that the jaw had not been anesthetized. My follow up question to the patient was " Did the anesthetic take effect?" No it had not! What had happened was that the skinny needle had been advanced too far and penetrated an artery. With a normal syringe you would know because blood would return into the syringe. That was why he and I both experienced some "event" and neither of us got the benefit of local anesthetic, during our dental work.

Sometimes after a vaccination or an infection, the immunological response targets the peripheral nerves. It is known as acute post infectious demyelinating polyneuropathy or Guillain Barre syndrome This results in progressive weakness and numbness in the extremities and even the facial and respiratory muscles. I saw a lady who had such symptoms. I went out to the nurses station to prepare the patient for transfer to the intensive care so she could be monitored more carefully for respiratory failure or cardiac irregularities et cetera. In the time it took to do that, about 3-4 minutes, she had developed complete paralysis of all 4 extremities. Despite treatment with immunosuppression she did not recover for about 2 months.

Months later I ran into a relative in the parking lot outside my office. She was most appreciative of the care her aunt had received. I was really pleased that she has entirely recovered from her weakness. The relative went on to say that she also suffered from an underlying psychiatric history and she was now completely incapacitated with psychosis.

One colleague had seen an elderly lady with headaches for years. After a while, she decided to get another opinion with me and on the very first visit I arranged for her to have a head CT scan. At that time, Computerized tomography was a new technology in the area. The test revealed that she had a malignant brain tumor.

Later I heard from the colleague's secretary who had met the patient in town, and she told me, the patient was maligning me bitterly, for not making the diagnosis years before and she would not be persuaded to the contrary . Many patients fear a brain tumor, when they have headaches and it sometimes quite difficult to dissuade them from doing an unnecessary test to exclude the diagnosis. What is the likelihood then , that a young lady in her 20's would have a headache as the presenting symptom of a brain tumor.? Not likely and it wasn't that she was demanding an unnecessary test but I did order a CT scan of her head on the basis of some concerning elements to the headache. She had a malignant brain tumor.

I believe it is the only time that a tumor presented in my practice with headache only. . In all the years, I do not recall a case, where I refusing to order a test, and missed something but there was an illustrative case I read about. The story related that a lady sought medical advice because of severe headaches and she was repeatedly told that her headaches were psychogenic "It's all in your head." Eventually she took a gun and attempted to commit suicide. Fortunately she survived the self-inflicted head wound and the subsequent testing revealed that a brain abscess had been causing her headaches all along.

A lady came to my office with headaches and was sent for a head CT scan which was normal. At the follow-up appointment, 2 weeks later, she had paralysis of one arm , and I asked her when this had happened. Apparently, it had occurred just after she left the office, 2 weeks before. She was sent straight back for another CT scan. In two weeks, the scan had completely transformed from normal to an extensive malignant tumor. In the days before MRI one trick was to give more iodine contrast and then delay the scan. Today with the massive data obtained from one MRI, it would have been found on the first pass.

A young lady with active Multiple sclerosis began to stutter and have difficulty expressing herself. Employing Occam's razor, I perseverated almost too long anchoring her current symptoms to her previous diagnosis but she actually had suffered from a stroke .

I think that praise and criticism are often equally misplaced. A case that comes to mind was a gentleman in his 40's who presented to the Emergency room with a resolving paralysis. A stroke workup was initiated because of the sudden onset of his symptoms, and by the second or third day, we had determined that he had a benign tumor in his heart called Atrial Myxoma, This a known cause of stroke as it sheds clot material, into the arteries, I was really happy to have identified the cause so quickly. This is a rare condition that neurologists know about, but may not see in an entire career. When I entered the room he was frowning and said curtly. "Everyone knows that atrial myxomas can cause strokes, you should have diagnosed this three days ago." So much for patient satisfaction!

A young lady came to my office with vertigo. Vertigo is the feeling we all experience as kids when we roll down grassy hills or step off a ride at the fair. She had had a low-grade fever and vertigo, but by the time of her appointment, she was better, Finding nothing of concern, I reassured her and sent her on her way. Only a few days later I happened to be on call and was paged to the emergency room. "We are not sure what is going on but the patient you saw the other day is having a seizure. " I rushed to see her and witnessed something I have not seen before or since. She was conscious and talking, then she suddenly arched her back, stiffened and lost consciousness, her pupils dilated, then she recovered for a short while, was able to communicate with me then went back into the same fit . The optic nerves were swollen. She was having "brainstem fits". We found a cerebellar tumor, which was compressing the brainstem. Fortunately she survived with surgery and radiation, and did well over the long term.

Neurologists are called in to evaluate the prognosis in a range of conditions causing coma. Mostly these are cardiac arrest patients, there are some drug overdoses, a few head injuries, metabolic causes, prolonged low blood sugar et cetera Normally the diagnosis is straight forward and requires relatively few basic brainstem reflexes to establish the level of coma. A confirmatory test for brain death is the apnea test. The patient's respirator is stopped and the CO_2 level is allowed to rise. It is CO_2 that drives the respiratory centers in the brainstem. Normally in the course of this test, nothing eventful happens, After some minutes have passed, the ventilator is reattached and the blood gas is determined . I had heard of the Lazarus syndrome named after the biblical story of the pauper, who was brought back to life by Jesus. A young lady in her 20's, was in the ICU and was, by neurological criteria, brain dead. I began the Apnea test, watching the time and her vital signs, when she abruptly flexed at the hips and sat bolt upright in the bed. We were all quite taken aback, It is hard to be nonchalant   when a brain dead patient sits up in bed!

Willis whose name is given to the circle of blood vessels surrounding the base of the brain, was a famous doctor of his time and he was probably best known by the Oxford lay public of that era, because he was involved in a singular story of resurrection or resuscitation. The story is outlined in " Eponymists in medicine" by Trevor Hughes

A certain Anne Greene became pregnant by the son of the owner of the house where she worked. She concealed the newborn child, which may have been stillborn, she was taken before the magistrate, found guilty of murder and hanged on the gallows in Oxford in 1650. After she was pronounced dead, her body was brought to the Anatomy rooms for dissection. When the coffin was opened she was found to be breathing and Willis and the Anatomist Perry successfully resuscitated her. She was later pardoned, became famous, married and bore three children. Willis and Perry who together saved her life must have acquired instant notoriety, as that story circulated in the Hay market.

An elderly lady was seen in the office several times for severe neuralgia following shingles. I tried several different medicines but none of them proved effective. She was very gracious though and kept coming back, trusting that if I just kept trying I would eventually find something for her. One visit she came in, looking terrible. She had all sorts of bruises and abrasions and she told me the following story. Her friend Mary died and she went to the cemetery to attend the interment and pay her last respects. The grave was dug and a brass railing assembled around the grave. The pall-bearers place the coffin over the grave and the railing are used to lower the coffin into the ground. After the coffin was settled in the bottom, she approached to throw some flowers into the grave, and as she did so , she tripped on the ornamental railing, fell into the grave, landing on top of the coffin . As she lay there she whispered to Mary 'I am not planning on staying down here, Mary." She was hauled out and an ambulance was summoned. As the EMTs arrived to pick her up, she said, "I bet this is the first time you have taken one out of the cemetery."

I used to see neurological consultations at Newport Hospital. It was not a very good arrangement (commuter neurology) but I did see some unique cases, including Martha Von Bulow.

Consult requests were typed on slips of paper and it was not always clear what the reason for the consult was. I entered the room of a gentleman with some kind of pain syndrome, and he enlightened me: "My balls ache." I told him that I thought the consult was intended for a urologist not a neurologist and I beat a retreat. About two years later, I got a second request for the same gentleman so I sought him out and entering the room, introduced myself. 'Hi I am Doctor Worthington ". "Yes I know" he replied." and they still ache !"

I heard many war stories from WWII vets. One in particular, was a gentleman whose abdomen was crisscrossed with a number of scars. He was a Paratrooper dropped behind the lines in Normandy on the morning of D day and he found himself alone in the cover of a hedgerow when he encountered a German soldier, the two were apparently armed only with bayonets and they set about each other in their own little private war, bayonetting each other until they were both thoroughly wounded. It seemed so brutal and mediaeval. I think I prefer Eric Newby's wartime story of an encounter with a German officer high in the Apennines. The German officer was collecting butterflies. Eric Newby was hiding out, behind the lines waiting for the Allies to arrive. The two went their own ways after a pleasant conversation.

I can envision that scene so clearly because I used to live above Marzabotto, close to where Eric Newby hid . I also used to collect butterflies in the Apennines. The profusion and diversity of the butterflies was spectacular. I can imagine these two gentlemen meeting on a warm dry day, in a high meadow with the background buzz of grasshoppers, surrounded by mountains in every direction. A nice pastoral scene of two gentlemen meeting in wartime, but an infamous massacre took place here, in the mountains above Marzabotto, in a village called Quercia. There is nothing there, but a neglected cemetery and when I drove up there, in the late 60's , I found rusty mortar fins and shrapnel sticking out of the mud .

The Germans had warned against hit – and-run attacks by the resistance, and when a soldier on horseback, was ambushed, they had had enough and slaughtered the entire village and razed the building. SS officer Walter Reder led the attacks around Marzabotto and it is estimated that 770 men, women, children and infants were killed during this murderous mission. He was captured after the war in Salzburg and imprisoned in Gaeta. Many years later, in the late 60s I heard via an Italian Naval officer, who had witnessed Reder at the prison in Gaeta, stepping out of his cell into the bright sunlit courtyard and make a Nazi salute. "Hell Hitler " before he exercised. He did this day after day. A little robotic Nazi, frozen in time.

I have been told about a young soldier who lost all 4 limbs during the war and was carried about in a basket after his return to the city, the proverbial "basket case". He was circulated from home to home by the married ladies in town, for a while. That is all I know about that story!

An older couple had appointments back to back, he had chronic MS and she had Parkinson's disease. He used Canadian crutches and she used a wheelchair. They sat in the waiting room together, then he wheeled her into the office for the visit. After the visit, she walked out pushing him in the wheelchair, much to the surprise of onlookers in the waiting-room. It would give one pause to be seen by a doctor who can make a wheelchair patient walk and put a walking patient in a wheelchair.

During rounds one day during my residency, we went to see an older lady with chronic headaches. As I stood by the bedside, with a junior resident and a couple of students, I asked how she managed her headaches.at home. She then grabbed a large bag by her bed and drew from it a huge chrome-plated industrial strength vibrator, and applied it to the top of her head as we applied our best poker faces.

Sometimes patients need, props to accent their illness. Unfortunately this often results in a lot of expensive hardware, cluttering their attics and consuming thousands of healthcare dollars . One lady with multiple sclerosis felt she should have an electric wheel chair. I disagreed and she promptly sought out her primary care doctor and waltzed off with a crisp new prescription. I never let her come into the exam room in her motorized wheelchair because it was too difficult to get the wheelchair into the small office, and besides she did not need it. She rolled up to the waiting room but had to get out of it and walk into the exam room without assistance. Eventually she tired of this charade and gave up the wheelchair altogether. That is a cure of sorts, I suppose.

Hary Janos, Baron Von Munchausen
and the good soldier Svejk

Early in my career, I was treating a young Portuguese lady, who had uncontrolled seizures. I would describe her meek and mild, until I determined that she was not having seizures but pseudoseizures. At the time I was inexperienced enough to confront her with the diagnosis. I did not realize how deep these issues go and I had basically stripped her of her emotional defense mechanisms. She immediately turned into a snarling she-wolf and I felt lucky to get away unscathed.

By the time I dealt with another patient who landed on my doorstep with continuous non-epileptic seizures, I knew better. These are difficult situations, particularly in public spaces because onlookers observe, what appears to be, ineptitude in the face of an emergency. Since she was not going to give up, an ambulance was summoned, and she was admitted for observation. By the time I got to her room, it was devoid of anything but a mattress on the floor. After a day or so, she announced that she did not need Dr Worthington anymore and left!

A gentleman I followed with numerous symptoms over the years, was seen in the ICU with a diagnosis of seizures. When I received the consult, I called back and assured his nurse that whatever he was doing, he was not having seizures. The nurses figured out after that, that he was actually holding his breath until his face turned puce. We just watched him until he gave up and gasped for air.

I have had patients show up in the ER with seizure-like episodes. The ER staff will administer lorazepam, a sedative, intravenously, to stop the seizures. The problem with this approach is when the lorazepam is the motive for the seizure. I got a call one night on one such patient and I urged the staff to stop giving lorazepam boluses for pseudoseizures. "If you keep this up the patient will go into respiratory arrest." 30 minutes later I got a consult to the ICU for "respiratory arrest " and had to drive back in to town.

An emotionally conflicted young man presented to the ER in a "comatose state." There are lots of little clues when the coma is a conversion syndrome. It seems he had reached breaking point in a homosexual panic and escaped into a world where the clamor of his family was neutralized .

There are new interventions for acute stroke, which basically require a protocol for rapid assessment and intervention . I was one of the first to actually use TPA, in the local hospital but there are many problems getting everything lined up on a timely basis and these days the evaluation is undertaken with the help of telemedicine . One of the first emergency evaluations was requested for a married woman with complete paralysis down one side. The crucial social history in this case was that she was in a bi-racial marriage and her mother-in-law was moving in, directly from the hospital where she had recently had both legs amputated.

During our medical careers, we all encounter, the " frequent fliers" and patients with bewildering histories that can create cynicism and frustration. There is a Portuguese term "agonia", which is all too easily assigned to older Portuguese ladies. My personal experience is that while depression is a frequent cause, I also learnt to be very circumspect about the term, as it sometimes masked very serious problems. Besides at its worst it was only a minor cultural difference, but has the potential to deflect attention from the real underlying problem. Then there were the factitious disorders such as non-epileptic seizures and then truly difficult Munchausen and proxy Munchausen syndromes. A young lady had a medical disability that precluded her escaping from her mother's clutches. I believe the dynamic was of mutual hatred, she was getting medical attention through pseudoseizures, despite also having real seizures and this, naturally, was disrupting her mother's life , but I was also certain her mother was withholding her seizure medications at times. They had each other by the throat and were doing this dangerous and destructive pas de deux.

A gentleman with a bewildering repertoire of symptoms, was prescribed chemotherapy for an ill-defined inflammatory disorder. He was expected to lose hair in this little experiment, but unexpectedly this did not happen. Then his wife asked me one day "Where did his hair go?. She woke up one morning to find her husband lying beside her, completely bald. No hair, nowhere. She simply did not understand how that could happen. People find ways to get through their lives in ways that are not comprehensible to observers, maybe like the Good soldier Svejk, they find a way through the maze of life, traveling a road that the rest of us , maybe, would not have taken. John Hills, a neurologist I greatly respected and tried to emulate, said "Remember that every hysterical patient dies of something real." Worth remembering!

I was by chance, passing by in the corridor, when I glanced in and recognized a patient I have seen for years . Envision this scene: it is a peaceful setting, an uncluttered room. The patient is lying peacefully at repose, eyes closed, to his right are lined up, in order of height, wife and three children to his left and with his back to me, the priest is delivering some sort of prayer or last rite . I entered the room, grabbed his big toe and said "Hey, Tony, what's up?" One eye snapped open and fixed me in his gaze, without responding. I guess, his time had not come yet.

Hardly a day goes by that I do not hear a patient telling me a story about how something happened, they ate something or they had a fever, then something else happened and the two had to be related. This is known as "Post hoc, ergo propter hoc". It can be quite distracting when a patient is convinced that there is connection. Unfortunately the Dunning-Kruger law applies here, particularly when it comes to vaccination. "My child developed autism right after his shots." This has been a real problem in society where a toxic disbelief in science and an almost religious state of post- hoc-ergo-propter-hocism, has resulted in parents refusing important vaccinations such as measles. There are outbreaks occurring in the US where it was essentially eradicated I would not wish it on anyone to have their child develop subacute sclerosing panencephalitis or SSPE, a terrible complication of measles. Actually the Measles vaccination case started with a scientific report linking Autism to vaccination. The doctor who wrote it was subsequently found to have erred in his analysis and was stripped of his license. An even worse story surrounding this vaccination paper is that the doctor was paid by a consortium of lawyers, who intended to make a huge financial windfall for themselves by suing the vaccine manufacturers. (nice people) Once uninformed people get hold of that sort of information, they run with it, heedless of the facts or the risk to their family and other members of their community.

Something evil, this way comes.

Something much more sinister lurked in the recesses of that old dingy ward at the end of the subterranean hospital corridors. A middle-aged man arrived at the emergency room with a range of ominous symptoms, including dizziness, double vision and vomiting. He stabilized and slowly improved. I used to visit him in the old twilight ward, until he was ready to be discharged. He did well and had only a little difficulty with his balance when he left. I was surprised that his nurses came to me, more than once and told me quite emphatically that I needed to get him out of there. as soon as possible They were not voicing a specific problem, more an intense unease in his presence. I certainly had no sense of anything unsavory at the time. The nurses were deploying their intuition warning systems. Six months later, he was back in my office with new symptoms and as I went over the findings, I was struck by the fact that they were not real. This is unusual. Someone with a previous stroke does not normally feign recurrence, though there could be motivation such as a disability application and I did wonder why he was malingering.

Not long after, he was jailed for the

murder of his girlfriend. In fact the alleged crime had taken place just before that office visit. After he was released on bail, he again returned to the office, claiming fresh symptoms and again revealing factitious signs. At that point, I felt obligated to send him for a second opinion in Boston. There they agreed with my impression but did not speculate as to the reason. In the end he went to trial and his attorney told me that I would be called to testify that he was too weak to have carried out the alleged crime. I indicated to his lawyer that my testimony would include terms documented in the record such as "malingering" and "factitious" and would be unlikely to help to his client's case. I think he agreed and I was never called to the courthouse. He was found guilty of murder. The postscript to this case was the receipt of a letter from his family explaining that if I had not denied the disability, I would have got the bills paid.

A man in his 20's who was seen regularly for some neurological problem, got himself into the local newspaper for assaulting a lady in the street and stealing her pocketbook. In the end, he moved on, sensing antipathy and his parting comment was "Talking to you is like talking to my lawyer"

A regular office patient, made the news print when she had a crush on a married woman. To realize her "dream" she planned to murder the unwitting husband, presumably hoping to sweep the distressed widow off her feet, Fortunately, that "dream" was never fulfilled.

Others were more successful in their hidden schemes. One weekend, I was at a small gathering in the neighborhood, when I was contacted by the police. It appeared that my office suite, at the professional building. had been broken into. There really was nothing worth their while, stealing, but I went into town anyway. Apparently two suspicious characters were seen in the building, one actually had a wired jaw, which I thought would make him fairly easy to identify. They jemmied the deck drawer (which is still broken to this day) and they labored to remove the hinges off a door that wasn't locked. This event may have had something to do with the disappearance of a medical record that was later to become important.

"What a tangled web we weave"

It just before Christmas, and I was on my Saturday rounds at Newport, when the pulmonary consultant, called me on the telephone. The gist of the consult was "There is lady here in the ICU who is an alcoholic, She came in unconscious and now has developed unequal pupils. "

I found her lying, comatose in the Intensive care unit. A nurse accompanied me to the bedside, as I did a quick assessment. Before I even got into the neurological testing to establish the level, of her brain function, I could see that something was very wrong. She had a split lip, facial scratches and other signs of physical injury. Pulling away the bed sheets revealed bruises and long scratches on her right leg. I turned to the nurse and said " This is highly suspicious." Moving on, I found, she had a low body temperature and the labs showed that she had a very low blood sugar. There was also a small amount of a barbiturate but no alcohol in the blood. Her exam was consistent with "mid to late transtentorial herniation". That in simple terms suggested the brain was swelling inside the rigid confines of the cranium. As this occurs the brain becomes distorted by the rising pressure, blood flow declines until the pressure inside is the same as the peak systolic pressure, then , there is no longer any flow of blood carrying vital oxygen and glucose and brain death ensues. If hypoglycemia was the cause, she would never recover but if low body temperature was, it might even have had some neuro-protective effect. Amobarbital, even at a toxic level would not have cleared from her blood and hers was not even up to the normal level, let alone a toxic one . Furthermore the half-life of this drug is 24 hours so if it was the cause of coma, the level would have remained well in the toxic range. In this case, the driving principle was one that I learnt in training at St Elizabeth's . A neurosurgeon was evaluating a young lady with a few outward physical signs of injury. She turned out to have two traumatic brain hemorrhages, and I asked him why he had zeroed in on trauma as the cause of her coma. He warned me, saying that if there are any outward signs at all, of trauma, you have to have a high level of suspicion that much greater mischief may be brewing within. Another tenet is: first assume the reversible worst-case scenario. A head injury might still be reversible but time was of the essence, if we were to save her. I immediately called her doctor and told him that with all the evidence of physical injuries hypoglycemia or not, we had to treat this as TRAUMA. His reply was bizarre and I got the distinct impression he was deflecting away from the possibility that physical injury was involved, His explanation to me, was that the injuries were from seizures. Disputing his reasoning was pointless, She did not have a seizure and I have never witnessed these types of injury occurring during seizures or resuscitation . I felt I had done all I could, because he was now stuck with my opinion on record. In view of what was to follow, I should have requested a medical photographer at that point. Arrangements were made to send her to Peter Bent Brigham hospital in Boston. There the team ruled out a bleed but concluded that she had suffered irreversible brain damage from a prolonged severely low blood sugar. The signs of trauma were documented. I was told later, that a medical student observed the same scratches, I had seen on her right leg.

I had no knowledge of the previous hypoglycemic episode a year before, nor the tests performed in New York that established that there was nothing significantly abnormal about her glucose metabolism., except a reactive asymptomatic low sugar in response to a sugar load on one occasion.

She had been in the ER a year earlier with unexplained hypoglycemia so a doctor, familiar with the case realizing this was a replay, made the correct diagnosis immediately and drew an insulin level.

As this tragedy was unfurling, and the brutal reality of irreversibility was setting in, her family developed a theory that pointed to the husband as the perpetrator. The suspicions had already started when he had behaved with cold indifference during the first coma. At that time her maid found her unresponsive in bed at 9.30 am. The husband was dismissive and seemed unconcerned and did nothing other than tell the maid not to disturb her, because she had been drinking the night before. It was not until that evening around 6 pm, that the maid, who kept monitoring her off and on all day, correctly determining she was unconscious, not sleeping. She became alarmed and demanded something be done as the patient had still not recovered and was now showing an ominous change in her breathing pattern . The Primary care doctor was finally summoned, and he arrived almost immediately to assess the situation and right then she went into cardiac arrest. He resuscitated her and she was rushed to Newport Hospital. By the following day she had recovered. It is not clear if she had any recall of the events leading to her hypoglycemic coma.

So now, this was a year later ,and we were dealing with the second unexplained hypoglycemic coma, an anniversary event, happening far from the big city hospitals in New York. The first episode was resolved at the last moment by the maid's vigilance and demand for intervention. The second episode occurred with the interfering maid, left behind in New York, leaving the victim vulnerable and unfortunately she was not there to intervene in the second episode. As a result, the low blood sugar irreversibly damaged her brain, destroying who she was, and in the process, leaving a human body capable only of sleep-wake cycles, eye opening, occasional yawning and automatic bodily functions , known for this reason as the vegetative state.

The first three physicians who attended her at Newport Hospital. all independently, suspected foul play. The only one who clearly did not, was the old socialite doctor who, in a letter two months following the first coma, actually expressed the belief that her husband had saved her life by calling him. This was same doctor who was telling me that all the injuries, I documented were attributable to seizures.

I moved on with my work, but rumors were soon swirling, that an investigation was underway by the Rhode Island State police. Finally the sensational story burst upon the scene and the husband was indicted for the attempted murder of his wife. The trial opened in Newport,

2 years after the second coma. The State had medical evidence that she had been injected with insulin which caused the irreversible coma. They also had a motive: money and sex. His girlfriend had no illusions it was about her, though, it was about a massive inheritance, the husband stood to gain in the event of the victim's untimely death.

I assumed that in criminal cases, the State Police would gather all the information and obtain depositions from all the people who were involved with her care. I believed it was only a matter of time, before I got a call asking me to explain the neurological findings and the implications of the various types of injury described in the medical record. I was nervous about having to appear as a witness. let alone, a sensational court case like this one. I think most normal people would be. It was with an increasing sense of relief, then, that as the trial ended, the call never came. In March 1984, the husband was found guilty of attempted murder, based on the medical evidence and circumstantial evidence of the witnesses and with the conspicuous motive : money .

The trial concluded with a 30 year sentence

It is never quite that cut and dried, though, for the rich, even if those riches are in reality, the victim's inheritance. He hired a new team of lawyers and was able to convince a Rhode Island judge to overturn the verdict on the basis of technicalities, not any substantive details.

The moment, the verdict was reversed on appeal, the reality was that the husband stood very little chance of getting a guilty verdict, second time round .   Lawyers, are millers of information. They grind kernels of fact with their grind stones until definable issues are rendered unrecognizable, homogenized and indivisible. After the appeal was upheld, the State prosecution was stuck with one narrative, while the Defense was able change the narrative completely and they did. As a result they were able to run circles around the prosecution and that is exactly what happened. Every single piece of evidence was challenged and by the time the grind-stone ground to its inevitable conclusions, there was really no reason for her to be comatose at all, just a series of medical and lab errors, no insulin, no motive.

Now for me the moral landscape had changed. Where I had been fortunate to avoid the exposure of "the trial of the century", I was now left with the very real possibility that he would be found not guilty. Anyone reviewing the medical record would, reasonably, ask why the evidence of bruises and scratches, a swollen wrist and a cut on her lip was excluded. Why was it never mentioned? At some point, someone could reasonably ask why I had not divulged this information. Being anxious about appearing in court, is not really considered a viable answer, in the court of public opinion, even if it is the truth. 4 years had passed and I remembered I had written something in the record reinforcing my concern. I was troubled by the attending physician's dismissive explanation to me, the consulting neurologist, that the injuries I had documented were from seizures. I had written "TRAUMA" in capitals because it would be something he would have trouble sweeping under the carpet, if he was ever challenged. It turns out I did not have copies of my hand written and typed consultations. The records had either disappeared from the office file, or the records department at Newport had sealed them because of the pending criminal investigation, but that seems unlikely as it was months later. I finally got to review them, when the State police investigator gave me a copy. I have subsequently wondered if there was a link between the missing file and the inept jaw-wired thief who, one Saturday evening broke into my office, but I really do not know for sure. It might just have been an odd coincidence.

I decided that I should make a preliminary telephone call to the Attorney general's office. " Excuse me , Um, may I speak

to the Attorney general." I couldn't remember
her name in the moment, which clearly irritated
the receptionist answering the telephone. I was
informed that someone would call me back after
I explained that I was one of the doctors involved
with the victim after she went into her final coma
.

Sure enough, I did get a call back from
the State police officer handling the case. He
came to the office for a deposition and my first
question to him was "What did you think I was
saying in my consultation?" He said that they
had noticed the description of the injuries in
more than one of the reports, but they were not
sure what to make of them and has not pursued
the issue. "Why would you not use all the
information in the medical record?" He told me
at the time and I was to hear this, more than
once, " We go to trial with the parts of the
medical record that the Prosecution and Defense
agree to, ahead of time , the rest is set aside." So
I had endured all that apprehension waiting to be
called to testify, for nothing.

The court proceedings are staged. It is not
Perry Mason. The script is finished before the
curtain rises. I was incredulous! It was
becoming quite clear that there was little room
for understanding between our different
professions. It was bizarre and inexplicable. I
enjoyed talking with the Lieutenant though, and I

think we both learnt something in the exchange, when he came to my office for the deposition. Strange how haphazard the process was, for a major criminal case, particularly if you contrast it against a deposition today, where the lawyer knows when you picked up the phone, what time you accessed the radiological studies and what time you reviewed the medical record. There are excruciatingly detailed time-lines documented in perpetuity. Completely irrelevant "stuff" that malpractice lawyers sift through, trying to create innuendo, they can feed to jurors, giving meaning to the meaningless.

He asked me if the victim had blood on her teeth and I remembered quite clearly that she did not. He explained that when she was transported to the hospital, her teeth were completely caked in dry blood. I would not have seen blood on her teeth because by then, she had been cleaned up in the intensive care unit I did not see her until the next day, so I never knew about this critical observation. When she was "found" by her husband in a comatose state on the floor of the toilet with a window open to the winter air, she was lying face down. There was no blood on the floor, when the EMTS picked her up. Again, the implications were huge. She must have spent many hours on her back, comatose, for the blood to dry on her teeth, yet she was found face down. I still cannot imagine why that would not be crucial evidence. No medical photographs, no evidence ?

I felt after the deposition that I had discharged my responsibility, and I felt I was all set, but my secretary's husband who was a senior corrections officer and more familiar with these matters disabused me of the notion " You are going to court. " and so it was.

In Providence, Trial of the century Take 2, was getting underway. Today if I mention the trial, most likely anyone 10 to 15 years younger than me, knows nothing about it. Trials of the century come around regularly every couple of years anyway.

My discussion with the Lieutenant, had ripped a little hole in the stage set. The judge was very inconvenienced by anything off script. If fact at the end she went quite a way to ripping up the script herself. I was asked if I could attribute the injuries to a struggle or altercation, otherwise the testimony could not proceed. I thought about it for a few seconds then replied in the affirmative, not that I had any interest in court theatrics.

There were a number of injuries from bruising to scratches down her leg or on her face as well as a split lip and wrist swelling. Even today we do not know who did it or why, but these injuries cannot be explained on any other basis, in the real world, so I was willing to say so.

The day I appeared in court, I was in the waiting area with the Neurologist who saw the patient after transfer to Peter Bent Brigham and we had a conversation about Music and the brain. His favorite composer was Mozart, mine, J.S. Bach. My theory about the difference is that we are hard wired for our composers. Studies appear to show that we are also hard wired for our political affiliations.

I relaxed by meditating a short while, in the waiting area and then it was time. I felt quite calm really. The husband had acquired a romantic "Klingon " while he was going through this ordeal, and she appears to have been very interested in writing a book about the entire sordid story. She noticed my "joyous little bowtie "as I walked "jauntily "into the court. Joyous ? She might have reconsidered the adjective if she knew the reason I really started wearing bowties. It had very little to do with joyous. There were some questions about my education as they were casting about for discrepancies. I went to school in Oxford England. The lawyers were trying imply that I was fraudulently claiming a medical education at Oxford University. The judge and Prosecutors and defense attorneys were all going through their choreographed waltz on stage, and then I showed up with a Putipu. (See Google!)

I referred to the prosecution as "my lawyer" instead of the "Prosecution lawyer", to the absolute delight of the defense team. Yes, yes, obviously, cannot be trusted, biased witness et cetera et cetera. It is like a Middle school debating society, they revert to such childish theatrics, worthy of Monty Python. The part I never understand is how the average person keeps on swallowing this sort of disinformation pabulum again and again and again.

The most illustrative moment occurred when one of the defense team needed to make a show of just why I could not possibly say what caused the different injuries. Split lip, bruises, blood on her teeth, they could deal with, but qualifying the scratches as being caused by nails was not part of the dance steps . The trial was taped and when I got home later, it turned out that at the very most critical moment, the TV program cut to an advertisement. I taped what I could on VCR, but later it was erased for some more pressing show like Sesame street. The jury had been moved out of the court to avoid having the script polluted by my testimony. The Judge asked me how I could tell if scratches were self-inflicted or not and I said that typically they would be short, parallel but might criss-cross. The defense attorney then approached the witness stand to test my acumen in abrasions and he wanted me to inspect something he had prepared. The Prosecution rightly objected for irrelevance and was overruled. It was the judge's opinion that he could proceed, and with a flourish, he rolled up his sleeve and there in perfect array were 3-4 parallel scratches all the same length and one crossing them. He had walked into a trap of his own making, The scratches were exactly what I had just a described to the judge. I knew it and more importantly the Judge knew it and he knew it .

Despite this the judge allowed him to continue with the charade .

"How did I get these scratches ? "

"I cannot say. "

That could mean "I cannot say" because I do not know but it meant was something entirely different . The judge knew, but did nothing, therefore I concluded she was overtly assisting the defense in blocking evidence. Would the lawyer have dissembled, had I declared that the abrasions were self-inflicted? Under the circumstances , I thought so.

" I cannot say ", actually meant :- " I am not going to say." because the Judge, the Attorney and I, all knew the truth.

Perception, not the truth, is king in court.

"What caused them?" They looked as though the could have made with a tongue blade or at the handle of a table fork, but really there could be a 100 different ways to create those abrasions.

"I don't know," I said, but I did know that they bore no resemblance to nail scratches. They have quite a unique signature. The lead lawyer thought him a veritable Perry Mason, but I do not find it surprising that he was described as being " unusually reticent" to discuss it afterwards, Good theatrics, bad ethics . I never was able to get the Video of that moment. Later that day when I got home, my wife showed me 2 scratches on one of the children," Well", I replied, "that one is a nail scratch! and that one looks like a scratch from a briar thorn." Both correct!

Later the defendant opined to his transient lady friend, "Anyway men do not scratch when they fight. " Maybe, but who said he was fighting with his wife. A much more plausible reason for scratches is that someone was trying to hold her down and she was fighting for her life.

The victim's husband, was a sallow, sinister looking gentleman, who was staring unblinking and intently at me at the witness stand, I don't doubt that he remembered exactly how she came by all those injuries. We had a little private I-can-out-stare-you duel and I stared back with even more malevolence until he was compelled to look away .

As I mentioned, at the second trail, absolutely everything was challenged , the Expert witnesses for the defense came up with a menu of different medical diagnoses, anything was good as long as it wasn't insulin, and the jury, reasonably enough, as the end threw in the sponge, . 'Not guilty"

The narrative, as controlled by the Judge, made no sense. There was a lady lying in a vegetative state in a New York Hospital requiring 24/7 care. How did that happen? No idea. Who did it? No one. The judge denied any financial evidence that would have shown how her death would have turned her husband into a multimillionaire overnight.

Why did it happen? "No reason." She played a large role by slashing uncomfortable evidence and received accolades from the lead Attorney, for her grande performance .

The story might instead have gone like this: the couple had tired of one another, Suffering the ennui of the socialites with first world problems and temperamentally ill-suited to one another. There are hundreds of pages written about their lives and motives and it is a tangled web indeed. He developed a fancy for the soap opera starlet, but there was a catch, if he left his wife, the wealth and life style would have evaporated and along with it, the starlet or any starlet, for that matter. The heiress is surreptitiously sedated at the dinner table. A little sprinkle of barbiturate in the red wine? .She retires to bed and he comes to her bedside later and injects her with a lethal dose of insulin. The Insulin takes a very long time for her to go into a coma. In fact the first time, he was hovering about, all the following day, watching her as the maid became frantic and finally under pressure, he summoned help. The heiress recovered and but had no memory of what happened, or did she? She refused to ever talk after that episode, about something that was troubling her.

A year later, it's Christmas in Newport. With the maid safely out of the way, in New York, he attempts a repeat performance, a little Amytal in the glass of red wine and a syringe-full of insulin. She is not sedated enough when he comes to give her the lethal dose, and she wakes and puts up enough of a struggle that he has to restrain her and she sustains cuts, bruises, scratches, swelling of her wrist. He is able to hold her down and slowly as her blood sugar falls, her resistance ebbs and she becomes cold, clammy, pale, and lapses into a coma, from which she will never recover. Hours later, she is repositioned face down on floor in that cold little room, next to the toilet, to await the arrival of the EMTs in the morning,   I am told that both EMTs had a feeling of dread as they carried her out of her home for the last time .

That could be the story but I don't have dog in this fight. The lawyers and the judge and pretty much anyone with no information at all, were very comfortable giving fact-free opinions. In this day and age, people are completely shameless about truthiness and fact-free opinions.

One of the New York lawyers opined to the Judge that " This case should not be the one for Dr Worthington to make his maiden voyage as an expert witness." I cannot help crack a smile when I hear this sort of comment. How do intelligent and supposedly quick-witted people make completely vacuous comments and not expect to be lessened by them? I did get a call at the office later, from a lawyer offering me an expert witness gig. My secretary answered " He does not do that." In the aftermath, an acquaintance said he deserved to get off, because money should be able to buy you freedom. Another friend felt she was fully entitled to say " It was the maid!" like a game of Cluedo? Somehow my involvement, the massive amount of evidence was irrelevant to her "right" to believe it was the maid. It seemed so alien at the time, but it is de rigueur today. Daniel Patrick Moynihan said " You are entitled to your opinion, you are not entitled to your own facts."

but nowadays fact-free opinions are a standard of the mainstream media and have even been "weaponized " on the right, to indoctrinate the voters and political focus groups. People do not vote against their self-interest by good old fashioned repression but by a continuous stream of low level indoctrination, or in more poetic terms "brain washing".

In this entire chilling saga, from the first coma, to the black leather photo-shoot of the husband and his Klingon lady published in Vanity fair, there are very, very few people who redeem themselves. The heiress died on a nursing facility, 28 years later. She is buried in Portsmouth Rhode Island.

Cold cases

Sometimes, there are extraordinary coincidences. Recently I attended a very informative lecture on the uncommon Arteriovenous fistula. These are direct arterial to venous bypasses that allow a direct connection between the high pressure arterial system and the low pressure venous system. As a result of this anomaly, a range of complications can occur. Seizures, bleeding, strokes, swelling. They are easy to miss. About 3 days after the lecture, I saw a gentleman in consultation, made the diagnosis and sent him to interventional neuroradiology.

Interventional neuroradiologists are an elite group of highly skilled experts who perform very delicate intravascular procedures, blocking aneurysm with wires, inserting stents and balloons and in the case of fistulas sealing off the feeding vessels. The patient needed some physical therapy for a short while, but had an excellent recovery. From lecture, to diagnosis, to successful intervention, it went like clock-work! Another lecture got me thinking about a case that I remember back 37 years before. A young lady in her early 20s was admitted with fever, confusion and we made a diagnosis of Herpes Simplex encephalitis This was a very dangerous condition with a significant mortality before the era of antiviral treatment. A few weeks after she was discharged, she was readmitted in an acute psychotic state. It was a remarkably florid presentation and I always wondered how this beautiful young lady developed a terrible complication that looked as though it would be only heartbreak for her family. I do not know what actually happened to her, but recently there was a lecture on NMDA encephalitis. Most of these are triggered by Ovarian tumors which contain immature brain tissue. The immunological response to the tumor also attacks the patient's brain. A bizarre and frightening neurological picture emerges. The patients may look "possessed " zombie-like or acutely paranoid and combative, On occasion, nurses have been so unnerved by their appearance, that they refused to be involved with their care. Occasionally this is complication of Herpes simplex encephalitis. The condition, though very alarming, is followed by recovery. So it may have gone well for her in the end after all. I hope so.

A lady suffering from a lymphoma, suddenly went blind, At the time the Attending physician and I did not find a reason for her blindness. Years later I was to learn of paraneoplastic syndromes which specifically attack the optic nerves or the retina. These diverse syndromes are due to the immunological reaction, the body mounts, to counterattack the tumor. This is another group of illnesses with dread manifestations and little we can do to help.

Diagnosis of convenience.

Among the worst of conditions, is locked-in syndrome. People became familiar with this entity, because of the movie: Diving bell and the butterfly. A stroke in the brainstem, just above the spinal cord, results in a frightening condition, where the patient is fully conscious but cannot move, talk or swallow. The only means of communicating with them is through their residual eye movements which are usually limited to 'up" and "down'. When a patient came into the hospital, Locked in, family members, petitioned to withdraw his care. I was the first to see the patient in consultation and in my opinion Locked-in is not one where substituted judgment is warranted, after all the patient is awake! If you take the time, you can communicate. The family wanted a second opinion and got the same diagnosis. So they went to court and the judge said that he could not back the families plan unless the patient was in a chronic vegetative state. The second neurologist reexamined the patient and went back to court and testified that the patient was now in vegetative state. The court backed the families intentions based on this and care was withdrawn. Maybe that was the best outcome but I would not make that judgment.

Sometimes the patient is on the knife edge and the decisions have to be made in minutes, treating the patient may shrink brain swelling bringing them back from the brink and I may "save" the patient's life but as a result, condemn them to a very low quality of life with severe and permanent disability and crippling costs to the family. Another time I was seeing a patient on the verge of death. The family had to make a decision immediately and there was no time for considered contemplation. With the families consent, I started treatment, but overnight and given more time to reflect, they opted to withhold and I think it was the right decision. One hopes the family are all in agreement on an end-of-life decision but difficulties arise when there is not consensus.

An elderly lady suffered from carbon monoxide poisoning in a house fire. One of the daughters was religious and because of her beliefs could not accept the poor prognosis. Her sister was medically trained and realistic about the outcome. As time went by, they shared in common, a dread of seeing me, coming down the corridor with my mantra of no hope. They decided they needed another neurologist. Maybe it worked better for all concerned but after 6 months she died without ever recovering. I heard that during those 6 months, the religious sister had become the pragmatist and the medical sister had found religion.   They had completely reversed roles.

A young man was seen in the office, for several years for traumatic brain injuries and seizures. He had been in a motorcycle accident and was disabled but was fortunate to inherit some money from his parents. At some point he started to tell me about small lottery winnings, at each office visit, just small amounts like scratch tickets.   Then came the jackpot, he had won more than a million dollars. He was very excited about it and told me the organizers were "on the way" from somewhere in Canada. I was very concerned naturally and believed he did not fully understand how to protect himself.   I congratulated him but at the same time, advised him to get legal advice right away. Ten days later, here was a notice in the newspaper, announcing his death. It turned out he had been scammed by online swindlers and lost everything and made a terrible, agonizing decision to end his life.

Another bad decision. This time it was a gentleman scratching out a difficult living, diving for quahogs in Narragansett bay. He had epilepsy and his seizures were not completely under control. I pointed out that diving was incompatible with seizures and he should definitely not do it. To make matters worse, he worked alone with only a rope attached to him to avoid drifting away from the boat, in the strong currents of the Bay. They found the boat drifting with the rope dangling over the gunwale.

Two young gentlemen, were seen in the office within weeks of each other. They both presented with seizures. One decided he did not want to go back to his previous occupation and looked to me to provide him with confirmation that he was disabled. There are restrictions when returning to work, Things included are, exposure to moving machinery, unprotected heights, roofing or situations where their co-workers could also be endangered in the event of a seizure I felt he was able to work within that framework. The other patient had a seizure and was exposed to unprotected situations. Though he wanted to go back to work, but because of his situation, could not be cleared by me. Both patients with the same problem, and both unhappy with the decisions, I made in each case.

My lying eyes.

When we are young, most of us believe, that what we see is reality, however it does not take long before we experience mirages lakes of water that disappeared as you drive towards them or the rainbow, with its promise of a pot of gold. I actually did walk along a farm road, after a beautiful rainbow when I was about 6. After marching earnestly along for a half mile or so, hoping to bring gold back to my parents, it dawned on me that this was not going to prove as easy as my eyes told me.

When I was in a lodging house, my first year in medical school, my roommates were Italians. Unlike me, they all rushed off for catholic mass and confessions at the church nearby. In the dim light of the church, their eyes began to wander, and settled upon two beautiful young parishioners. Somehow, by employing universal signals, they arranged to meet these eligible young ladies later. After sprucing up, several of them left on their quest. An hour or so passed and they returned somewhat deflated. What was up, I enquired. " La Luce fa brutti scherzi."   (Light makes bad jokes).

What is the world like when, the world you see is entirely generated from within? I have had several patients with a dementing illness called Diffuse Lewy body disease. One of them lived the last of her days with constant, horrific hallucinations, which I could not control and it was anguishing for her family to watch her suffering so much.

The Parkinson's disease population frequently have minor hallucinations. They understand that it is related to their medication and the most common seems to be of someone sitting in their car parked in the driveway. They can be much more troublesome and one gentleman had a hallucination of his spouse, engaged in a sex orgy, on the sofa in front of him. Sometimes, a whole family will appear tp troop through the sitting room, silently, all of them less than half normal height.

The most common visual hallucinations occur in elderly patients with poor eyesight, the brain making up for missing visual input .

I have encountered a few patients with an uncommon visual hallucination known as "peduncular hallucinosis" They may have undistorted vision but colors are completely wrong . People's faces may appear in bright primary colors, One lady saw a green background and little cartoon giraffes all over her hospital room walls and ceiling. It lasted for weeks.

Sometimes the visual problem is not recognizing what you are looking at, as happened with the lady who did not recognize her own clothes in the closet. Sometimes it is the opposite, the patient is blind but claims to be able to see. One gentleman recovering from open-heart surgery was seen for a visual disturbance. He seemed to be able to see individual objects in the room such as the TV but he did not follow with his eyes or maintain eye fixation and could not reach for objects placed in front of him. Fortunately as happened frequently in a post-op situation, he recovered quite quickly. I have been told that if you wear glasses, that invert your vision, you will, after a couple of weeks, start seeing right side up again, The brain flips the image for you. but when you stop wearing the inverting glasses it takes a another couple of weeks for the vision to revert back to normal . From time to time I have seen patients who complain that their vision has suddenly inverted or tilted and I interpret this to be in the brainstem with potentially serious consequences.

Our eyes are not cameras, it is quite possible to not see things, right in front of you, ask any married woman! On a serious note though, I believe that many accidents involving cars and motorcycles are due to of agnosia. If we are looking for a car we may completely eclipse the motorcycle, coming towards us, One time I was turning out of a side road. Dutifully looked left, then right then left , nothing coming, and as

I started to pull out there was a tap on the hood. A group of men was jogging right across the road in front of me. Not even a dirty look or an expletive, they had probably encountered this sort of thing regularly. You often hear people say after an accident, that they never saw the car coming. I think that is not an excuse, that is what they experienced,

It is not uncommon to see confused patients in the hospital, who in the course of assessing them, it transpires that they believe they are in bed in their own home. In one unusual case, an elderly gentleman was accompanied by his daughter, to the office visit . He was proving to be a frustration to his dedicated daughter, who was caring for him. He kept telling her, she was an impostor and that he was not in his own house. His house was down the street and he would constantly take off to find his home and his real daughter. Now this is not uncommon in Alzheimer's disease, but other than suffering from this strange delusion, he performed well with memory testing. During the visit, he started to work his delusion on me, insisting that if only I would pay a visit to his home, I would understand. It brought to mind The Rolling Stones lyrics: " I tried so hard to rearrange your mind, but after a while I realized you were disarranging mine."

Bad decisions do not always point to

Alzheimer's disease, however much the family may wish it. An elderly gentleman was seeing a lady, decades younger than himself and spending the requisite amounts of serious money on her. His daughter was convinced that there could be only one explanation: Alzheimer's disease. After examining him and asking questions about his decisions and their possible consequences, I understood that he was fully competent to make his own decisions. I fully understand why I would not have got a good "patient satisfaction " rating on that one. The daughter marched out of the office, volunteering to everyone in the waiting room, how useless I was.

A more poetic insult perhaps, came from a middle aged lady, admitted to the hospital for testing. After examining her, I concluded she had relatively trivial neurological problems. She did not take the news kindly. She sat in her bed, arms crossed, glaring at me "I don't believe you"

" No problem," I replied, "you can always get another opinion, that is fine with me ." As I was writing up the consultation, a nurse came running "She is getting dressed, she wants to leave. She called you a fricken quack."

I have no explanation for the next story, but it disarranges my mind. Once I attended a garden party where a magician was hired to do magic tricks. He was not your Tommy Cooper.

The guy was brilliant and the tricks came so fast and beyond comprehension that after while I just became inured to the inexplicable. This story is like that; Two ladies came to the Emergency room at the same time and were admitted and two consultation requests were sent.to me. The first lady was Portuguese " Maria Ferreira " the second lady was American born in the city. "Helen Smith ". The patients were placed on different floors and after I finished the consult on Mrs Ferriera, I hopped up the stairs to see Mrs Smith. The second patient had suffered from a stroke and was having great difficulty expressing herself. I usually start by asking their name and she replied very slowly and hesitantly " Ma-ri-a F-err-iera" As the words were slowly enunciated, I already knew the name she would give before she finished. She could not say her own name. When I recount this some people try to rationalize that they must have known one another or that there was some exchange in the ER, I must have been mistaken but the majority react the way I did to the magic tricks, It just doesn't make sense so they dismiss it.

Dystopia's spiral

After 38 years of a Neurology practice, I still found every day to be a challenge. I have mentioned the attempt to link the quality of care to reimbursement. It eventually dawned on the new medicine architects, just how difficult it is to do that. They could, however pick the low hanging fruit and that boiled down to the fairly meaningless value of "patient satisfaction " This included such parameters such as the doctor's courtesy, timeliness, the length of their wait All things that can be easily converted into data, while having absolutely no relevance to patient care or outcomes . The architects of value-based reimbursement, do have some other measures in the works, but from what I understand, these are items like maintenance of certification. If you drill down into the structure, these include Practice improvement and advanced care information. The problem is that doctors are already burdened with the responsibility and work load of their profession to the point that their own quality of life is quite degraded. The planners, are increasing the irksome requirements while pushing punishment as the incentivizing factor. I do not believe working practitioners could possibly have any input in the planning and I do believe that most of it will do nothing to improve actual care. I do approve of curtailing profligate spending but have yet to see any effective controls. At the same time, indiscriminate Prior authorizations are yet another bludgeon. As for "maintenance of certification", doctors are already required to maintain continuing medical education and I personally feel strongly that, it has helped me provide better care to my patients over the years. Maintenance of certification, appears to be much less about improving care, than monetization, for the benefit of the certifying organizations. Neurologists are mostly diagnosticians, and looking back, I found that my patients mostly needed reassurance, which helped and comforted them the most. The counter to reassurance was that if you could not offer them reassurance, they went away with foreboding. Even when people develop serious illnesses, they can somehow deal better. when they can have a clearer vision of the scope of the problem. The unknown can be more terrifying. With the current time constraints, there is a greater tendency for doctors to order expensive testing and referrals. This creates a larger volume of unnecessary diagnostic tests, particularly with MRI imaging. The problem with MRI is that it is such a good tool for visualizing the soft tissue of the central nervous system that it frequently reveals abnormalities that are irrelevant to the clinical presentation. The unwitting patients are told all manner of information, quoted verbatim, from a radiology report. The report, naturally, has to include a broad differential diagnosis for the clinician to consider. I have heard numerous times, about patients being given a diagnosis such as " brain tumor", during the course of a brief emergency room visit. What is left out of this exchange, because of exigency, is that this "tumor" may be benign, small, and may have been there for 15-20 years and may never affect their health in any way (other that the intense anxiety that must inevitably follow statements such as "you have brain tumor") There is enough time to read out the results , not enough time to go into the details.

One doctor would, without examining the patient, tell them their diagnosis. To one of my patients he announced "I know what you have", wagging his finger at them, he conferred upon them a diagnosis of MS. So more than anything else, patients were immensely grateful to hear that their problem was minor or irrelevant. Sometimes I will read the report to them and say " What do you not understand about the statement " tiny and nonspecific" They sometimes said I had granted them a new lease on life. So, regulators and insurance gnomes, how do you measure the value of that?

Commiserating with me about the changes taking place in the delivery of healthcare a Boston neurologist, I was consulting with, said, "What other job could you do at your age and still be challenged every day?" It is true, but the old ways of the profession are vanishing and there are probably many people who are happy to see it dismantled. The Primary care doctors have largely retreated or been banished to their offices. The new doctors are "hospitalists", employees of hospitals or agencies. Their job is to process patients and get them discharged within the required number of days designated by their "code". If a patient stays longer, the hospital loses money. If they are discharged before the assigned number of days, the hospital gets to keep the difference. They are essentially " Discharge technicians". This has lead with clockwork precision and predictability to increased readmissions, which is another cause for Medicare finger-wagging and fines. It is an extraordinary concept when I never see any two patients alike and yet they can be coded into exactly the same pigeon-holes. I think anyone reading about the readmission problem, would say, " Well that was predictable, wasn't it?"

I have reviewed orders in a patient's chart and found the order for a CT scan and Neurology consult, 3 times on 3 consecutive days, despite there being no change in the patient's condition. I think the hospitalists were so busy during their rounds that they turned on their heels and wrote orders without spending the necessary time to analyse the situation themselves.

As a specialist, there have been very significant changes. There is no longer a primary care doctor, familiar with the patient, taking care of his or her hospitalized patients. There used to be robust communication back and forth between us, these were my colleagues. The primary doctors had followed the patient and other family members for years. Nowadays consultations are flung out like confetti, even before it is established whether there is a neurological problem. Any number of times, admitting orders included "Consult neurology, consult psychiatry". Tests are ordered with abandon. In recent years, communication has also degraded between hospital staff and consultants. I have frequently arrived at a nurses station, to consult on a patient, only to be told that the patient had been discharged already. Several times I have made an hour-long round trip for nothing. Sometimes a patient with a Bell's palsy (facial nerve paralysis) has been admitted and subjected to extensive testing MRIs Ultrasounds Echocardiograms, blood work, et cetera, costing thousands of dollars , for a benign condition . All of this done, before seeing a consultant, who could have saved the patient a lot of inconvenience and the insurance, a lot of money. Bell's palsy for example, most of the time, will resolve on its own, without any treatment   I had a patient one time that I saw for multiple cranial nerve palsies, a condition known variously as Painful ophthalmoplegia, Tolusa-Hunt Syndrome. This is a self-limited condition responding to steroids.   The gentleman did actively seek medical advice elsewhere, but because I presented the case at rounds I tallied up with reasonable accuracy the approximate cost of his testing (not including doctors' fees) $52,000. Recently I heard that the number of CT scans for a diagnosis of "headache" is increasing despite the fact that it has been established for years that CT scan of the head has a very low yield for finding relevant underlying pathology. There are two reasons I think this happens. Ordering a test takes a lot less time than listening to the patient and examining them carefully, besides the patients are a lot more comfortable being told their CT scan is normal. The second reason is that there is very little motive other than personal integrity for doctors to withhold unnecessary tests. I do not know what the current British N.H.S. environment is but I expect there is a lot less money wasted on unnecessary testing, because there is no motivation to do so in

Britain or Canada. The insurance companies know the doctors habits, but they have little control over referrals and the patients simply do not know and are not incentivized either. People tell me that Single payer cannot work in the US, because patients will overuse the system. Are we willing to say that we cannot get a single payer system up and running because we, as patients only care about our individual wants and that the government cannot be trusted to provide for us when we need the care? I take issue with the faceless bureaucrats in the Government, who have dreamt up the dreadful dysfunction that pervades our system. Granted it is a work in progress, but it is not leading us to new and greener uplands of good medicine for all, but a sort of punitive dystopia, in which the doctor/clerks have to buy expensive computer programs that consume more time for almost every patient interaction. These expensive electronic medical records need a lot of personnel to support them, they are fraught with bugs and errors and need constant attention and updating. Even a 30 second call from a patient becomes a maze of clicking and writing, but if you get the sequence wrong , you have to start again. If you do not do all the little "meaningful use " items that have almost nothing to do with good care, you will find a menu of punitive consequences. Despite the consults written in the record being available to the referring doctor, the government regulators have decided that the consultant has to send an E mail along with the actual report known as P to P. Reason: there's not to reason why, but I checked and found it took numerous mouse clicks (9) and more wasted time to achieve this mandate. Now here is the thing. The computer has all the necessary information to do this automatically, if it were actually useful. You can call it C to P if you are so inclined, but why burden and frustrate the very people you need to provide the care? More and more mandates keep coming down from above. I read recently that the Meaningful use program has been recognized as useless and will be changed, and here is the kicker, Medicare will go back and review 6 years of meaningful use records, to see if you met the standards and they will fine doctors for insufficient compliance with a system they already admit does not work and which is being replaced. I am still trying to get my head around that insanity .

Read the ICD 10 codes to get an idea of this byzantine coding system. I find the "second encounter with a lamp post" not entirely inappropriate for where I trained in Chinatown with Pine Street just down the road, but " subsequent encounter with Jet Engine?" "bitten by tortoise?" well, Ok, I have been bitten by tortoise with a toe fetish. but "struck by a tortoise ", takes it to a whole new level! Ten different codes for encounters with parrots? Maybe, for each finger, they lacerate ?

ICD10 the current coding system, did not have a code for Ebola, when that highly infectious disease burst onto the news cycle, which pretty much says it all. There seem to be a lot of people out there who are steering the ship of healthcare with neither knowledge of healthcare nor navigation skills. I think these are the same people who brought us "Imperial life in the Emerald city",(*by R. Chandrasekaran*) after the fall of Baghdad. The hospitals and offices have to keep changing or upgrading their electronic medical records and all of this takes a lot of money, time and training and the cost and time falls largely on the doctors' shoulders. Prescribing in the electronic records can be extraordinarily frustrating and difficult. There is the inevitable joker in the pile: After spending 20 minutes trying to fill out a hospital prescription, something which could be written in 20 seconds, I was advised by the Pharmacist that I needed training to use the system properly. The next day, having a moment, I popped down to the Pharmacy department for my "education" and as soon as I explained the issue, I was informed that the computer program had a "bug" for prescribing this particular medication and they had not been able to correct it yet.   The last straw for me is interference by Hospital administrators in the appropriate delivery of medical care. They have their fiscal rules and I have my medical rules, their rules trump mine, that is, unless there is a lawsuit! That is when you will discover that you, the patient advocate, are responsible to ensure the safety of the patient not the administrators. It is all too Kafkaesque!

While there are doctor villains, most doctors are being coerced by forces beyond their control, into becoming medical clerks and scribes. The real villains are the health insurance companies with the capricious and ruthless hardball they play, the politicians who protect their interests and the Pharmaceutical industry. The Hospital administrators are minor league but villainous enough to qualify as Salai (Leonardo Da Vinci's pupil and lover)

I am an anachronism, a dinosaur practicing in the new age Medicine, from an era where the guiding principle was to provide the patients and family with concise information so that they can understand and control their management decisions. I am convinced that big data and insurance will for the foreseeable future be the guiding force in health care. It is not a pretty sight. My overriding impression and that of many patients, is that the current reforms are more about big business than actual care. Today, perhaps it is just as well that people seem to prefer comfort and happiness anyway, over truth and beauty. There is a huge upwelling of anti-science in the Nation. All those that went before and showed us the way to better medicine and scientific knowledge, no longer seem to be relevant. The anti-vaccination crowd believe it wiser to circumvent vaccination and have " measles parties ". It may not go well.

Hippocrates had something to say about science that is entirely applicable today:

"There are, in fact, two things, science and opinion; the former begets knowledge, the latter ignorance" In this era of truthiness, anti-science, anti-Vaxxers, fake news and the death of critical thinking. it has me wondering: Would I be the proud holder of a larger investment portfolio and a bulging file of " patient satisfactions", had I become a snake oil salesman ?

It has all gone by so fast, from academic wakening with Andrew at the Zoological station in Naples, to the University in Bologna, where I learn how to study. The fairly brutal dive into the hospital wards in England as an intern, and the more training-centered hospital life in the US. The realization that I was temperamentally suited to hands-on clinical neurology, and less so, the academic world, and the last phase: practicing adult neurology, which challenged me right up to the last day. I don't have misgivings because I was lucky to have my career during a relatively stable period in the profession where the skills, I was taught, were still valuable, and valued by my patients.

A few people question my decision to retire at 70. I could not go back now, the ground rules have changed and metastasized beyond my ability to adapt to today's demands. I came from a long line of physicians, on my father's side, but I am the last of my family to do so.

www.ingramcontent.com/pod-product-compliance
Lightning Source LLC
Chambersburg PA
CBHW071313200626
46813CB00015B/1809